To Valerie,
Enjoy!

The True Father

STEVEN ANDERSON LAW

[signature]

2-11-2012

YUMA, AZ

For my boy, Tegan. God's greatest gift.

Goldminds Publishing, Inc.
1050 Glenbrook Way, Suite 480
Hendersonville, TN 37074

The True Father

ISBN 10: 1-930584-29-6
ISBN 13: 978-1-930584-29-7

Originally published in paperback under the title Rodeo Summer by
Goldminds Publishing, June 2006. Second paperback printing
September 2008.

Author and cover photographs © Ron McGinnis.
www.ronmcginnis.com.

PUBLISHER'S NOTE

Printed in the United States of America
Signature Book Printing, www.sbpbooks.com

www.goldmindspub.com

"There is a universal structure to the western novel that goes beyond the call to adventure, the journey into the deepest, darkest cave, and it is this: The hero's search for his true father."

—Jory Sherman

The True Father

ONE

I expected to experience a deeper sense of fulfillment after completing four years of college. No more late nights cramming for midterm or final exams, or bickering with professors over the clarity of their test questions. And I had already lined up that "perfect job" at a downtown Kansas City accounting firm, with my own private cubicle and reserved parking space. According to the Dean, my professors and classmates, I had done everything right to earn it. The proof was right next to my name in the commencement program: Trevor Hodge, Magna cum laude, National Honor Society, Dean's List. A model grad, I was told, with a special gold rope hanging over my shoulders and down the front side of my commencement gown to prove it. But where was this foretold sense of satisfaction?

Here we were, nearly one hundred salty graduates organized alphabetically in neatly arranged plastic chairs, our brains stuffed with four years of formula and debatable business theory, all anxious to set foot into the real world. And now, our last task, to listen to the Dean's commencement speech that no one will ever remember, just so we can go on to that perfect job.

All I had to do was glance down the row behind me at Ernie, my best friend during this four-year trek of the brain, to suddenly realize why it all seemed in vain. He was there through it all— the midnight oil, the long journeys across the campus parking lots, the good and bad test scores, and the hops and barley celebrations afterwards. But now, for Ernie and I, it was so long. Rather than putting all this new knowledge to work he chose to give three more years to law school at the University of Michigan. He wasn't from around here so it was unlikely that we would ever see each other again. Plus, like I had told him, there's something about law school that takes all the affability out of people—a bar exam and one huge something or other up their ass to make them forget about what's important in life. Because we were friends he always took the teasing well. But in reality we both knew that after today it was good-bye.

After the ceremony, I gathered with my family for pictures out in the lawn in front of the campus recreation center. My mom seemed exceptionally proud, wearing out my smile with two rolls of thirty-six-exposure film. She took at least a dozen with my maternal grandparents who drove up from their Arizona retirement retreat just for me.

There was Mom's boyfriend, Walter, a Kansas City entrepreneur she had been dating for a grand total of three weeks. He was rich and she liked that. She also thought he was cute. I thought he was a penis head.

There were several photos with my two aunts and their husbands, plus cousins, friends, neighbors, and a few with Amber, my significant other for the past year. She was a semester behind me but in the same accounting program. We had studied a lot together, and were workout partners at the campus fitness center three times a week. So you might say we were more friends than lovers. We cared deeply for each other but mostly all we had in common was a keen understanding of Generally Accepted Accounting Principles. And for some reason our dinner conversations over this topic rarely had enough spice to lead to romance.

Ernie joined me for a couple of memory photos before Mom handed him the camera to take our picture together. During one of the poses with Mom I noticed a man behind Ernie who stood slightly to the left watching us. Mixed with the many people in the lawn, from the men in suits and neckties, the women in dresses or pantsuits, to the students in commencement attire, this man clearly stood out. Under the shade of a straw cowboy hat was a swarthy face that seemed rough and leathery. His bodily features were exceptionally thin, especially his legs, which bent awkwardly in faded blue jeans. A large oval belt buckle glistened in the sunlight. And on his lanky frame he wore a white short-sleeved western shirt with a bolo tie.

"Mom, I think that guy is staring at us," I said.

He acknowledged my observation of him with a nod and a touch of his hat brim.

"Oh my God," Mom said.

"What?"

"What on earth is he doing here?"

"Who is he?"

"He's—your uncle."

The only uncles I ever knew were my mom's two brothers in-law, and they both stood to my right drinking punch from the complimentary commencement refreshment table. So before I could ask her for more information, this cowboy she called my uncle started walking toward us. As he drew closer, I took a keen liking to his friendly smile, one that seemed earnest and polite, much different than the one our Dean had painted on for all his graduates. And when he approached, he looked at Mom and greeted her by name, and then at me, and he knew my name as well.

"Jeremiah," Mom said. "What a surprise."

"I'm sorry for barging in like this," he said. His voice was somewhat gravely but genial. "I went by your house. A fella across the street said Trevor was graduating today. I keep my tie in the glove box just for such emergencies."

Before I could wallow in any more confusion, Mom introduced me.

"Trevor, this is Jeremiah Hodge. Your uncle."

Being that his last name was the same as mine, I quickly assumed he was my father's brother.

"Why are you here?" Mom asked.

"Well, this is a tough one, Bonnie. And I hate to deliver such news, being a special day and all."

"What news?" she asked.

Jeremiah looked at me, his Adam's apple moved up then down as he swallowed, then shared again that gentle smile. "It's Jettie. He was killed two days ago."

Jettie was my father. I never knew him and knew very little about him, but I did know his name. It was rarely spoken, in fact, I couldn't remember the last time. All I ever knew was that he was a loner, a rodeo man, who resided somewhere in Oklahoma and all year long traveled the rodeo circuit. I don't remember ever seeing him, nor had I ever seen a picture of him. All I knew was that he was a man Mom wanted nothing to do with, and whom she said we were better off without.

"I'm sorry," Mom said. "What happened?"

"Oh, you know Jettie. I swear that man had more balls than brains. We all told him to stay off them bulls, that he was too old. But he would never quit, and he hopped up on ol' Cyclone down in Fort Worth. It wasn't pretty, Bonnie."

I didn't quite know how to feel, except when Jeremiah looked at me, he released with his eyes some sort of mystic compassion that held me captive.

Mom sighed and grabbed my hand.

"Well, I'm glad you came, Jeremiah," she said. "But you could have called."

He pushed his hat up and bowed his head. Several strands of sweaty gray hair fell across his forehead. "Yeah, I tried that but they said your number was unlisted. All I had was an address on an old letter, one that I found in Jettie's house. It was returned several years ago."

He pulled a letter-sized envelope out of his shirt pocket and unfolded it. It had yellowed from age, and the address was handwritten in blue ink, which looked like writing from a fifth grader. And just below the cancelled stamp was a blotch of red printing that read "return to sender".

Jeremiah raised his eyebrows at both of us, then folded the envelope and put it back in his pocket.

"I'm sorry about that," Mom said. "But why now?"

"Well, the funeral is in a couple days. Maybe you'd like to go."

"Oh, I don't think so—"

"What about the boy?"

"I doubt Trevor would be interested. He didn't even know Jettie."

"Jettie was his pa, Bonnie."

From her silence, I could tell Mom didn't know how to respond to this bit of truth. And from the sincere look on Jeremiah's face, I began to feel that he was on more of a mission than simply a bearer of sad news.

"I don't know what to say," Mom finally said.

"You don't have to say anything, Bonnie. The funeral is in Spiro Monday. It's at the Methodist church—you know, the one where you and Jettie were married."

Along with the same smile he arrived with, Jeremiah pulled his hat back down, nodded at both of us, wished me congratulations then turned and walked away. I had never seen a man walk the way he did—sway more than strut, as if his legs were stiff and permanently bent. And even as he walked away, there was a certain power in his presence. More so than the excitement of commencement day or the news he came to share.

But as I looked at Mom, as she watched his departure, I could see a look of fear in her eyes.

"Are you okay?" I asked.

"Ah, yes. I'm fine."

"That was strange, huh."

"Yeah, well—thank God he's gone."

TWO

Our house was a small English Tudor styled bungalow in a quaint area of town, not far from the Country Club Plaza. The Plaza, as it was commonly called, was built and maintained by the affluent of Kansas City. To be associated with it, or live anywhere near it, meant you were either rich or moderately wealthy. We were neither, but Mom liked to hint that we lived that way, which also explained why she dated guys like Walter.

Inside and out, every chair in our little mansion was taken. The entire family showed up, including Walter, along with several friends and neighbors, even some who didn't come to the commencement. The patio was a popular place, but the shyer guests—whom I assumed just came for the free food—hid inside. A few settled for one of several folding chairs that Mom brought up from the basement or rented from a party store, while others chose to stand. But wherever they sat or stood, they ate. Each held a small plastic plate full of food, and somewhere near them, a clear plastic cup filled with either pink punch or beer. And though this was supposedly the opulent section of town, we weren't opposed to serving tuna fish on pumpernickel rye, cocktail sausages out of a crock-pot, or Bud Light out of a keg.

Amber and I nabbed a couple of the folding chairs and took them out to the patio. She wasn't much of a drinker so she chose the punch. But I had an acquired taste for beer, one developed with Ernie the first semester of our freshman year, and tested almost every evening since. Today that acquired taste prompted a peculiar craving.

"So aren't you excited?" Amber asked.

"About what?"

"Everything. Look around you. This is all for you. It's your *big* day."

"Oh—yeah."

"Is something wrong?"

At first I wasn't sure whether it was the commencement—being the proverbial "kicked out of the nest" day—or whether the visit from Jeremiah made me feel the need to escape. But I didn't tarry long with the thought. Jeremiah's visit stunned me. Before he came everything was in place. My degree, my new job, all that I had worked for. But now I stood on a great platform of uncertainty, wondering what this whole day was about.

"Amber, we're pretty good friends, wouldn't you say?"

"Of course."

"But I've really never told you much about my personal life, have I?"

"No, I guess not. But you could start if you needed to."

She smiled tenderly, stood her cup of punch on the patio floor then held my arm with both hands. She looked different than usual. At first I thought it was the yellow sundress and white sandals. But then I realized her hair was down, shoulder length and in a bob, rather than up in a clip. And she wore a different lipstick and eye shadow. She was a natural blonde, petite with fair, olive skin. A thin face with oval shaped glasses that gave her a sophisticated look. She wasn't what most would expect to see on the cover of *Cosmopolitan*, when more likely, I could visualize her on the cover of *Fortune*—the first lady executive to be paid more than the average male CEO.

"I received some unexpected news today," I said.

"What news?"

"My father passed away."

One of her hands moved to my shoulder. "Trevor, I'm so sorry."

"It's okay, I never knew him."

"How did you find out?"

"My uncle—his brother—came to the graduation today."

"Was that the guy in the cowboy hat?"

"Yeah."

"So how are you feeling?"

"Weird as hell."

"What can I do?"

"I don't know. Just hang with me, I guess. I might need you later."

She smiled tenderly again. "I can do that."

Just as I was about to give her a hug Walter walked up and, with his fist, delivered a light punch to my arm.

"Congratulations, Champ."

He reeked of Tommy Hilfiger cologne and, dressed in an olive suit and a black knit shirt, looked more like a playboy than a businessman. Unlike the other guests, he carried a wine glass half full of champagne.

"So when do you start the new job?" he asked.

"Monday."

"You know, I belong to the same racquetball club as one of those VP's at that firm. What's it called again?"

"Bennett and Dobbs."

"That's right. I hear they have a great reputation."

"I hope so."

He returned a plastic smile, one that I was sure he borrowed from the Dean of business. "You know, if you strike out down there, you're always welcome to come and work for me."

I tried to act excited. "Oh, that would be cool."

"But that's just if you get into a pinch."

"Thanks, Walter."

He punched me on the arm again. "Don't mention it, Champ."

As he walked away I rolled my eyes at Amber. "Will you kill him for me?"

She laughed then stood. "I'm going to get some more punch, would you like anything?"

I handed her my glass. "I could use another beer."

"Sure—but don't get used to it."

"No way."

As she walked away I glanced around the patio. I noticed my grandfather visiting with my uncle, Todd. My uncle, I thought. Not by blood, but by marriage. This made me think again of Jeremiah. How interesting it was to see him. To have such a small taste of a life I never knew.

I watched my grandfather talk and express with his hands; a short portly man with a bald head and only a little white hair above each ear. I laughed at his attire. He couldn't wait to get home and get out of his suit and tie and into his one-piece jumpsuit—a godforsaken piece of light blue polyester with an elastic waistline and silver buckle, one that Grandpa always praised as being the most comfortable damned garment he ever wore. And he also bragged about his home, the one parked beside our house, a thirty-six foot Winnebago Chieftain that he and Grandma drove all over the country, especially during snowbird season.

I didn't have to watch him long before he noticed me, put my uncle on hold and came to me. He patted me on the shoulder and sat down in Amber's chair.

"How you doing, Trev?"

"Pretty good, Grandpa."

"You know I seen you talking to Jeremiah today."

"Hard not to notice him, huh?"

"Yeah, here in the big city old Jeremiah stands out like a pink bow on a pig. I wanted to say hello, but he got away before I had the chance."

"Did you know him?"

"Know him? His pa and I were best friends growing up. Yes, old Basil Hodge was quite the cowman."

"Cowman?"

"Sure, you remember that I used to be in the cattle business?"

"Well, I knew you had a farm down near Joplin."

"Farm? Hell boy that was a ranch! Fifteen hundred acres of the best damn ranchland in the country! Hell, when you was a youngun' you'd come down and ride horses every summer."

"Yeah, I remember that."

"You looked a lot like your pa when he was young."

"So I guess you knew him, too?"

He put his hand on my knee. "Yes, Trev, I knew you're pa real well. In fact, I loved him and Jeremiah as my own. Basil died and both them boys ran off and traveled the rodeo circuit. I wanted Jettie to inherit the ranch, and he would've if your mom and him would have stayed married."

"What happened to them?"

"Don't rightly know. And even if I did I don't think I'd be the one to tell you. But I do know one thing; your pa loved you. And I hated to see you all separate."

Like Jeremiah's visit, Grandpa's bit of history added fuel to these unexpected feelings. Jettie Hodge, a man my grandpa loved. A rodeo man. A man I never knew. A man who loved me.

"Grandpa, I've been thinking about the funeral. I'd like to go, but I start my new job Monday."

"Well, Trev, I ain't going to tell you what to do. But it's unfortunate that you never got to know your pa, and I think it would be good for you to go down there and see what he was all about. Go down before they give all his belongings to Good Will, and what's left gets blown away in one of them Oklahoma twisters."

"But what about my job?"

"The death of your pa isn't a good enough excuse to get some time off?"

"I guess it is. But I never knew him as my dad."

"Good God, kid, they don't have to know that."

"I guess they don't."

This time he slapped me on the knee. "Sure they don't. In fact, if I can talk your grandma into it, we can fire up the Winnebago and go down tomorrow, and you can ride with us."

"You don't have to go to no trouble, Grandpa."

"No trouble, Trev. In fact, I'm kind of looking forward to seeing some old country and old kin."

Amber returned with our drinks and Grandpa stood to give her back her chair. He teased and flirted with her like he did all the young women, then went back to his conversation with Uncle Todd.

"You doing okay?" Amber asked as she sat back down.

"Yeah. Had a nice talk with Grandpa."

"He's a neat old guy. I especially like his taste in clothing."

I laughed at her joke then looked at the patio floor. I kept thinking about Jeremiah, the funeral, and now Grandpa's offer. What would my new boss think if I didn't show up the first day? Was it worth the risk if he didn't approve? All I knew is that I couldn't stop thinking about Spiro, Oklahoma, a place that in just a few hours had more magnetism than a job I had worked four years to get.

THREE

I was anxious to get away from the party crowd so I talked Amber into a Saturday night movie, then a couple beers at a bar and grill, and later to her apartment where I spent the night. For Amber and I, nights like these didn't come very often. It took a special mood, our minds had to be far away from school or anything related to our career goals. This night happened to be one of those nights, when all I could think about was an upcoming funeral and the decision I needed to make by morning. Luckily Amber was there for me.

I sat up in the bed, my back against the headboard and sheet up to my waist. Conditioned air blew from a vent above the bed and felt good on my bare chest. I looked down at her as she slept on her side, her hands cradled over her breasts as she took in the breaths of sleep. I envied her ability to rest so peacefully.

I looked out the window and into the parking lot where the moonlight reflected off the windshields of cars. Though I couldn't see the moon, I could visualize it in my mind—an object so distant but powerful, with the ability to reflect the sun's light to the earth. It made me think of my father, and a family I never knew, and like the moon their images hovered in a distant space and drew me with an intoxicating force.

Amber and I had talked a lot about my decision, my sudden feelings, and the guilt I felt for not having these feelings before now. If not for her, I may have wallowed in self-pity the entire night, but she was just the pragmatic type not to allow that to happen. Now more than ever, I was grateful for her friendship, knowing that I could never have confided in Ernie with such a dilemma. He and I were best friends, but our common bond was more college buddy and a line seemed to be drawn there and never crossed. Another sign that the party days were over and the real life had begun.

I rose from the bed, put my clothes on and leaned over and kissed Amber on the forehead. I didn't want to wake her, but I couldn't possibly leave without leaving a little gracious affection. She squirmed a bit, but continued on in her quiet slumber.

I drove my car to the Plaza, parked and walked to where large fountains spewed under blurring streetlights. The night faded as a hint of coral light teased the eastern sky. I stood by the statue of Seville lights, where water poured from the mouths of theatrical faces, then to the fountain of the Greek god, Bacchus, and then my favorite, the three Heroic Horsemen. Though the horses reared and the horsemen raised their arms in battle, there was something serene about their presence—a freeze-framed image of a great defense, along with water that flowed around the horse's feet, sprayed into the air, and created a cool mist that went aloft and trickled on my face. I grabbed some loose change out of my jeans pocket, found a quarter and threw it in the fountain pool, joining it with the many other coins that rested in the basin. I didn't know what to wish for, but in a way I knew I needed strength to carry on my decision.

*   *   *

I wasn't sure how Kyle Bennett would respond to me calling him at his home early on a Sunday morning, but he was very sympathetic and told me to take all the time I needed, that the job would be there when I returned. He did, however, ask for a letter of verification from the funeral director. He said he'd need it for my personnel file. A bit odd, I thought, but like my grandpa often said, these days a man's word is virtually worthless.

I opened my closet door and looked at the half-dozen new suits that Mom bought for me at Saks Fifth Avenue. They were a graduation gift that she put on her Saks credit card. She wanted to be certain that her son looked his best, and no matter the cost, fit in with the downtown crowd. After I had tried on at least twenty suits, we settled on six conservative, perfect for accountant ensembles. There were two grays, one a solid charcoal and another a lighter shade with a faint pin stripe, a navy blue windowpane plaid, a khaki tan, and a dark three-button olive. Then there was my favorite, a black on gray glen plaid, the "banker's suit", I called it, which I'd planned to wear on the first day of the new job. But for the time being, I only needed one appropriate for a funeral. I knew it had to be between the charcoal and the navy, and finally selected the charcoal. It was dark and simple.

I lay it on the bed, and also from the closet grabbed a white pinpoint oxford dress shirt still in plastic from the one-hour laundry. Now came the tough part. Selecting the tie. The task at Saks never ended at just selecting the suits. The shirt selecting was easy—all white, but I was definitely a novice at matching ties. The salesperson was a pro at it, and he had given good advice. But I had nearly panicked.

"How am I suppose to be able to do this matching in the morning before work," I had said.

"Simple," he had said. "Burgundies and reds are a great contrast with any navy, gray, or olive suit."

So with his crash lesson in mind, I found a tie with a dark burgundy background and small black and white diamonds throughout. I lay it on the charcoal suit and became instantly impressed with my selection.

I wrapped the tie around the suit hanger and along with the shirt placed them inside a zipper garment bag. And inside a black duffel bag, I stuffed a pair of black dress shoes, black socks, and two days worth of casual attire for the evening after the funeral and the drive back to Kansas City the next day.

As I zipped the duffel bag I heard a knock on my bedroom door. I looked up to find Mom standing in the doorway watching me.

"Hi," I said.

"So you're really going to do this?"

"Yes, I am."

"Why?"

"Why not?"

"Trevor, you are risking your new job and all you've worked for, for something you know nothing about."

"Yes, and I've been wondering about that."

"About what?"

"Why I know so little about my father."

"There's not much worth knowing."

"You say that, and all through my life I've believed that. In fact, I was raised not knowing the difference between having a father and not having one."

"Then what good will it do to go down there now? He's dead, Trevor."

"And what a tragedy that is. Now I may never know who my father really was."

"Why this sudden interest? Did your Grandpa put you up to this?"

"No. Something tells me I need to go."

"I see."

"You know, you could help me a little."

"How?"

"I've never known what happened between you and him."

"You wouldn't understand."

"Try me. I'm not a child anymore, Mom."

"But why now?"

"Why not? Are you trying to hide something from me?"

"No, Trevor. Just consider the consequences of what you're doing. What possible good could all this knowledge of the past do for you?"

"Answer some questions. Explain some feelings."

"Like what?

"Well, for instance, what my dad was like."

"He was a loser. Does that help?"

"To you he was a loser, but lately I've heard nothing but good things about him."

"Believe me, Trevor, nobody was closer to your father than I was. All he cared about was that damned rodeo. He let a good job at a factory go just so he could go out there and get bucked off those stupid bulls. And wouldn't you know, it finally killed him."

"Oh, I get it. So he threw away a job for the rodeo and you think that I'm going to go down there and do the same."

"Well, I will certainly pray that you don't."

"I'm not going to lose my job, Mom."

She stared silently at my garment and duffel bags, then at me and let out a lengthy exhale. "Just don't believe everything those Okies tell you," she said.

"How bad could it be?"

"Nobody ever understood why I left Jettie. Many of them hated me for doing it."

Suddenly I felt less confrontational and a little sympathetic. I gave her a hug. "You know I'll never hate you, Mom."

She hugged me back and kissed my cheek. Tears welled in her eyes as she looked at me and rubbed my cheek with her hand.

"Be careful down there, okay?"

"Please, just respect my decision."

"I guess I'll have to."

FOUR

he day was sunny and bright, but a gale from the west had Grandpa cursing and struggling to keep the Winnebago on the highway. I sat in the passenger seat while Grandma sat far to the back and read a romance novel. I imagined that she sought out a spot that was not only comfortable, but as far away from Grandpa as she could get. He enjoyed retelling stories of his cattleman days, the rich land along highway 71 where his ranching operation once thrived, with an occasional interjection of "...damn that wind..." or "...that gust was a son of a bitch!" He was in his usual form, jumpsuit included, only today he wore one made of denim. I was amazed to learn those things came in a variety of colors and fabrics.

The drive south had lasted two hours before we stopped at Judy's Cafe, a truck stop in a little town called Jasper, Missouri. It was only ten in the morning and my sausage and egg McMuffin hadn't even digested yet. But Grandpa insisted that we couldn't go by Jasper without stopping at Judy's famous truck stop. Hungry or not, I had to admit I'd never had a better piece of apple pie in my life. It was fresh and homemade, and I learned firsthand what made Judy's famous. Nevertheless, I also had never eaten so much food before noon and it made me feel sluggish. Back in the Winnebago I reclined the seat, and while listening to another ranching story, I drifted off to sleep.

Next I knew I was sitting in an office cubical, punching numbers into a ten-key calculator. I was wearing my favorite suit, the glen plaid, and next to the calculator stood a picture of Mom and I at the graduation. Suddenly someone entered my cubical and tossed a piece of paper into an in-basket on my desk. I expected to see a copy of a spreadsheet, with more numbers for me to manage, but I picked up the glossy paper, turned it over to find a photo of a cowboy riding a bull in a rodeo arena. Frightened, I turned quickly to look behind me but saw no one. I looked again at the picture then someone else entered my office and threw another photo into my in-basket. I turned to find a clown smiling down at me. He wasn't an ordinary clown, like one at a circus. He had the painted face and the red nose, but he wore a ball-cap, cut-off bib overalls, black and white striped socks, and Nike athletic shoes.

He left the cubical, then another clown entered, this one wearing a cowboy hat, a yellow T-shirt, wide rainbow-colored suspenders, and torn and ragged oversized denim shorts. Rather than put a photo in my basket, he handed me a trophy. It had a long wooden base, and on top a golden statuette of a man riding a bull. I grabbed the other photo in my basket. It was of me with a man in a cowboy hat who stood with his arm around me. We were both smiling, but I didn't know the man.

I stood from my chair and walked out of the cubicle. I came to an abrupt halt as a crowd of people started cheering and clapping at me. There were the two clowns, and several men in cowboy hats and jeans. Then I saw Jeremiah, my grandpa, Amber, Ernie, and my mom, who wasn't applauding, but standing with her arms crossed. I tried to walk toward them but I couldn't move, and suddenly I felt a sharp punch on my arm. I turned to find Walter smiling at me. "Hey, Champ," he said. "Did you finish those reports I asked for?"

I didn't answer him, so he hit me in the arm again, harder this time.

I rose quickly from the seat of the Winnebago to find Grandpa slapping my arm. "Mother Mary, Trev! Wake up and look at that view!"

I rubbed my eyes and gazed out at a scene of rolling mountains, covered with green, plush looking trees.

"Where are we?" I asked.

"Arkansas. The Boston Mountains. Pretty, huh?"

The view was breathtaking and having just woken from a very weird dream, I wondered if I wasn't in some sort of a freak paradise.

I grabbed a plastic bottle of spring water I had bought at Judy's Truck Stop and squeezed several streams into my mouth. The water wasn't very cold, but it was wet and soothed my dry, cottony mouth.

We continued to wind down the interstate through the mountains until we came to a spacious river valley. Eventually the mountains faded behind us and we turned right and headed west, crossed the Arkansas River, drove through the town of Fort Smith, Arkansas, and on across the border to Oklahoma. The scenery was much like what we had left in Missouri; flat farmland with cattle and horses, but with a distinct difference in the color of the soil—a red-orange rather than black. And to the south, a hazy image of a lone mountain peaked up on the horizon.

Within minutes we came to a bridge that stretched over a small lake. Just before the bridge stood a sign that read "SPIRO BEACH," and next to the beach, a campground.

"That's where we'll park the RV," Grandpa said. "But first I'll drive you through my old stomping grounds."

The tiny town lay just on the other side of the bridge. A sports complex with several baseball fields and a rodeo arena marked the burgh's entrance.

"Right there's where it all started," Grandpa said.

"What started?"

"Rodeo—and the life of the Hodge boys."

The arena was nothing spectacular to look at. Similar to a high school football stadium, it had a section of bleachers on one side and a press box for the announcer. The press box was a small, wooden structure with weathered white siding, shaped similar to an old outhouse Grandpa had pointed out on a farm back in Missouri. A fence made of metal pipe, painted white and rusty in places, stretched completely around the oval arena. And on one end were several gates with fenced areas behind them—that Grandpa called chutes.

Grandpa continued. "First it was calf roping and bulldogging. Then they started bronc riding; both saddle and bare back. Then it was bulls. Nothing but bulls."

"Why bulls?"

Grandpa laughed at this question. "At first I thought it was peer pressure. Boys around the rodeo like making dares. But I soon learned that it was a natural thirst for competition that drove the Hodge boys. Man against beast. Your pa and Jeremiah both thrived on drawing the toughest bulls."

"Is there good money in rodeo, or bull riding?"

This also made Grandpa chuckle. "Only if you're real good. Most people these days work a day job during the week and run the circuit on weekends. Only the best make a living at it."

"But I understand that Dad—Jettie—made a living at it."

"Yes, but barely."

"Why barely? Was he good?"

"Trev, your pa had the talent to be one of the best."

"Then why wasn't he?"

"I doubt anyone knows that answer. I'm sure your pa didn't even know. It just seemed that he couldn't put it all together."

"What about Jeremiah? Was he good, too?"

"Not as good as Jettie. Jeremiah was Jettie's biggest fan. But he got frustrated over the years. Got tired of waiting for Jettie to make that big break."

"So what does Jeremiah do?" "Stock contractor. Provides animals for the rodeos. Around here, nobody knows rodeo or rodeo stock better than Jeremiah."

We turned off of the highway onto Main Street. It was a typical scene of a once thriving little town, now shut down by large discount outlets and convenience stores, and replaced by local ma and pa craft shops, hair and tanning salons, or buildings torn down into vacant lots. It resembled a scene in a documentary I once saw called *The Death of Main Street*, and what one of my college professors called " ... part of the evolution of free enterprise". I had never taken the time to draw my own opinion, but my first impression was that Main Street in Spiro struggled for signs of life.

Main Street ended at a railroad track and came to a T. A train approached and sounded its horn. I was amazed to see that the large gray engines were labeled "KCS" which I knew stood for Kansas City Southern, a railroad company based in Kansas City, and their office was in the same building downtown where I was to start my new job. How small of a world could it be, I thought.

Grandpa swung the Winnebago wide and turned right at the T. Though the business district of Spiro seemed run down and dying, the residential areas seemed alive and peaceful. Most of the houses were small, one-story structures, with either brick or wood siding. A few yards were mowed and tidy, where others were decorated with old rusty cars or broken down appliances and tall weeds growing up around them. At one of the homes an elderly man sat on his front porch in a lawn chair. He wore a red cap and striped bib overalls, and his eyeglasses had thick lenses making his eyes seem large and blurry. He held a fly swatter in one hand, and what looked like a glass of iced tea in the other. Grandpa waved at him, but rather than wave back, the old man swung the flyswatter at something on the porch rail.

"Interesting town," I said.

"Yeah, they're a dying breed," Grandpa said.

We continued on, passing a large school with a parking lot full of big yellow school buses, then on out into the countryside, where pastures covered with spring grass spread flat as far as my eyes could see. A short ways out of town, a white metal fence, similar to that at the rodeo arena only whiter, lined each side of the blacktop road. We eventually came to a driveway on the left side of the road and Grandpa swung the big motor home into the lane. At the end of the drive was a long one-story brick house, and out in the pasture grazed several horses and cattle.

"Whose house is this?" I asked.

"This ranch belongs to your Uncle Jeremiah."

FIVE

s we pulled into a circle drive in front of the house, the front door opened and out walked Jeremiah. Except for the absence of the bolo tie, he looked like he hadn't changed clothes since I'd seen him at the commencement. He even wore the same friendly smile. And not far behind him was a woman who appeared to be a few years younger, with short brown hair and wearing a T-shirt and blue jeans.

After the three of us climbed out of the RV, Jeremiah introduced us to his wife, Jodie, whom I learned from Grandma was only four years younger than Jeremiah. Anyone who didn't know would never believe it. Grandma said that along with smoking and drinking, Jeremiah's many days in the Oklahoma sun had aged him to where he looked over sixty. And she was right; standing next to Grandpa, who pushed seventy, Jeremiah could easily pass as his brother. In contrast, Jodie could almost pass for thirty. She looked fabulous, wearing skintight Wrangler jeans, lace-up cowboy boots, and a T-shirt advertising the 2000 National Finals Rodeo. In actuality she was the same age as my mother, forty-five, but I'd never seen my mom in such apparel, which possibly helped with the youthful image.

They invited us to their back patio, which was a large wooden deck made of treated lumber and coated with a water seal that made it shiny. A propane barbecue grill stood next to the patio door, and along the outside rails were several pots with an assortment of pink and white flowers. We gathered around a table shaded by an umbrella, and Jodie brought out a tray that held several glasses of ice and a clear glass pitcher of lemonade with pulp and lemons floating at the top.

"I'm sure glad you came down, Trevor," Jeremiah said. "For so many years I've wanted to get in touch with you. I'm just sorry it had to be under these circumstances."

"Me, too."

I could tell that there was a lot on Jeremiah's mind, more than just me coming to pay my last respects to my father. Something made him edgy and I had absolutely no idea what it could be, or what possibly I could do now to help.

Grandpa smacked his lips after taking a drink of lemonade. "I showed Trevor the old arena. A lot of old memories there."

"Yeah," Jeremiah said, "Jettie and I both ate our share of dirt in that old oval."

They continued to share ancient memories along with a few laughs—stories that I found fascinating to say the least. It was as if Jeremiah lived in a different world, with so much freedom and depth. Growing up in Kansas City I grew used to the sounds of automobiles on concrete and the smell of their exhaust. Everything that occurred in our lives took place in and around our little mansion, which set on less than a half-acre. Our social life centered on events with whom-ever Mom was dating that week, with all the promises of a family lifestyle somewhere down the road. I never realized it until now, but we seemed to be boxed into our own little world stricken with limitations. While here, one could listen to birds sing without the background noise of motor vehicles. All the land that surrounded us Jeremiah owned. And the stories of the past centered on events shared with their family. I tried to think of something to share about my past, but I couldn't. I had never experienced anything compared to the adventurous lives these people lived.

"So, I hear you're gonna be one of them big city accountants," Jeremiah said.

"Guess so," I said, wondering how my planned career measured up to anything he had done.

Grandpa decided to brag a little for me. "Yeah, Trev was one of the best in his class. Gonna be sitting for the CPA exam this fall."

"Sounds like you've got a good plan," Jeremiah said.

"I hope so."

Grandpa chuckled. "Jeremiah, you know what CPA stands for, don't you?"

Oh no, I thought. Not this joke again.

"Sure," Jeremiah answered. "Certified Public Accountant."

"No," Grandpa said, already laughing. "Certified Public Asshole!"

I think Jeremiah already knew the punch line but, if so, he played along and laughed anyway.

Finally Grandpa suggested it was time he take the RV down to the campground and get it set up, then Jeremiah insisted he hook it up next to his machine shop behind the house. They didn't argue long before Grandpa agreed to his accommodations. And Jodie suggested I stay in one of their spare rooms rather than in the RV, and after thinking of a night with Grandpa snoring, I gladly accepted.

While Grandpa and Grandma set up the RV Jeremiah invited me on a tour of the ranch. I followed him inside the machine shop and to his pickup truck, a white GMC with a black flatbed and dual tires on the back. From out of nowhere a short-legged, silvery blue spotted dog with pointed ears ran into the machine shop and jumped up onto the flatbed. Also on top of the flatbed was a tire mounted on a silver wheel and two bales of hay, and a guard made of square steel tubing covered the back window. The dog laid down next to the tire and rested its chin between its front paws. The bottoms of the pickup doors and rocker panels were splattered with a dark green substance that I managed to get on one of the cuffs of my jeans. At first I thought it was grass, like from the bottom of a lawn mower, but the closer I looked, I realized it was cow shit. Jeremiah grinned and told me I could give my jeans to Jodie and she'd wash them for me. I looked down at his jean cuffs and noticed they were free of manure stains. He assured me that the next time I climbed into a ranch truck I'd know better.

As we drove off through a gate and into a pasture behind the machine shed, Jeremiah pulled a pack of cigarettes out of his shirt pocket. They were Marlboros in a red and white package. He knocked one out of the package, stuck it between his lips and lit it with a plastic butane lighter.

He took me to all four corners of his land, showed me the boundaries, the land he hayed, his horse and cattle herds, and the bulls that he contracted for the rodeo. Not far from the bulls was a small pond shaped like a triangle with rounded corners. Two tan-colored birds with long white tails screeched and hopped in the grass near the pond. And as the bulls grazed their tails swatted back and forth to their flanks, and flies swarmed around their eyes and the sun-dried manure on their rumps.

Jeremiah stopped the truck and killed the engine. He pushed the cigarette butt into an ashtray, which was already nearly full with older butts, then lit another.

He shook a second cigarette halfway out of the package and held it in front of me. "You smoke?"

"No, thank you."

"Good for you."

He dropped the cigarettes back in his shirt pocket, opened the door and stepped outside. I looked out at the bulls, that now stared at us, and wondered how quickly the mammoth looking beasts would charge me once I stepped out of the truck.

"They won't hurt you," Jeremiah said.

Regardless of his assurance, and my trust in him, I opened the door cautiously.

Jeremiah leaned the seat forward, grabbed something wrapped in a small brown paper bag, then closed the door and came around to my side. He set the brown-bagged object on the back of the flatbed then lifted himself up and sat with his legs hanging. He patted his hand beside him inviting me up. I inspected the side of the bed carefully for more manure, then lifted myself up between him and the dog. I reached over and scratched the dog behind the ears. It closed its eyes and seemed to enjoy the affection.

"What's his name?" I asked.

"*Her* name is Jezebel."

"Interesting name."

"Yeah, a cattle buddy up by Tahlequah gave her to me, said her name was Lady. I got her home and within a week she had screwed every dog in the neighborhood. She had a litter of pups, half Redbone coonhound. Ugliest damn things you ever saw. So I had her fixed thinking that would help. Stopped the pups but it didn't stop her from whoring around. So I said the hell with it and changed her name to Jezebel. It's a name I can live with."

"What kind of dog is she?"

"Blue Healer."

I kept scratching behind Jezebel's ears, feeling somewhat sorry for her having such a label. "Are all Blue Healers so promiscuous?"

"Hell if I know. They're mostly known for their ability to work stock, and she does that well, too."

"I suppose if she does her job, then she's entitled to a little recreation afterwards."

Jeremiah chuckled a bit and folded down the top of the paper bag. He unscrewed a cap from a bottle, removed the cigarette from his lips then tipped the bottle up to his mouth. He took two swallows then handed the bottle to me. "Snort?"

I was hesitant, but I'd already turned down one of his generous offers, and besides, I liked a shot of whiskey every now and then. So I accepted the bottle, tipped it up, and like Jeremiah took two swallows. The fiery sensation afterwards took my breath, caused me to choke and wheeze, and I suddenly wondered if I was going to die right there on the back of the truck.

Jezebel apparently drew a concern for me and raised her head and barked. But Jeremiah told her to hush and, dutifully, she returned her head back to its resting position.

"You all right?" Jeremiah asked, almost laughing.

I nodded and continued to wheeze.

"I guess it's just one of those things you have to get used to," he said.

"What is that stuff?"

"Oh, just a little potion a fella down near Talihina makes for me."

"Potion?"

"Yeah, I don't care much for that watered down stuff they sell at the liquor stores. I like my booze to have a little kick to it."

"Kick? I think it took the skin off my tongue."

He laughed a little. "It'll grow back."

Still feeling the pain, I couldn't find any humor in his joke.

"You know," he said, "Jettie and I had our first taste of corn whiskey together. I reckon I was about fourteen. Your pa would have been ten or so. We were fishing the Arkansas River one night and before we left we found our pa's bottle and brought it with us."

"Well I hope you about choked to death like I did."

"We didn't take as big a swallow as you did."

"You could have warned me."

"I suppose I could have. But I will say we sure were sick puppies the next day. Drank the whole bottle. And pa whooped us good."

He handed the bottle back to me. "Best to keep going if you're ever going to get use to it."

"No thanks. I think I've had enough internal tissue loss for one day."

He put the cap back on the bottle and took a large drag off his cigarette. Then he retrieved something else from his pocket and handed it to me. "I want you to have this."

It was the letter he showed my mom and I at the graduation. I accepted it but didn't quite know what to say.

"That's not the only one," he said. "There's more down at his house."

I read the postmark. It was dated January 18, 1978. Back then I would have been a year old.

"More were returned?"

"Yeah, there's a dozen or so in a shoebox down at Jettie's place. After he died, I went down there to see if I could find a way to get in touch with you. That's all I could find."

Other than the sound of Jeremiah unscrewing the bottle cap, we sat for a moment in near silence. I studied the letter again. The address was the same as where we lived now—our home for the last twenty-two years.

Jeremiah continued. "Tomorrow afternoon, after the funeral, I'll need you to come with me to the lawyer's office."

"Why?"

"For the reading of Jettie's will. From what I understand, he left you some things."

"He did? Like what?"

"I have no idea. But we'll find out tomorrow."

Now my head felt as if it was spinning. Along with two gulps of homemade whiskey burning my throat and boiling in my stomach, I had this new knowledge to absorb. My father, who I never new, included me in his will, and left behind a shoebox with several more returned letters. But the one in my hand was at the peak of my interest. For some unknown reason, I couldn't find the courage to open it, as if when I tore through the paper something horrifying would jump out at me. With those thoughts in mind, I folded it along the age-old creases and put it in a back pocket of my jeans. When I looked back at Jeremiah, he tipped the bottle again and took another healthy swallow. Suddenly I realized that he hadn't just offered me a drink, but probably thought I could use a little valor as well.

SIX

While Jeremiah retired early, Jodie showed me my room and offered a closet for me to hang my garment bag. Never in my life had I met someone so hospitable, graceful and content. Everything she did, from the preparation of the lemonade to the fine barbecue supper that evening, was done with such great pride.

I straddled the edge of a leather sofa in their living room, which was connected with the dining room and kitchen, making it feel like one spacious area. The floors in each room were hardwood, and the walls were a textured white throughout, with paintings and artwork of the American West. I took particular interest in a painting hanging behind me, of a cowboy that rode a bucking horse. The detail was incredible, but more so the action and culture that it portrayed. The artist signature in the lower right hand corner read "Frederic Remington". Apparently they had an affinity for his work, because all the paintings on their walls bore his mark.

On the far end of the living room was a large stone fireplace with a matching hearth. Several photographs of various sizes and frames stood propped on the mantle.

Jodie walked into the kitchen and opened the refrigerator door, grabbed two beers and brought one to me. It was straight Budweiser in a longneck bottle.

"Can I get you anything else?" she asked.

"No, thanks. But I appreciate everything."

She sat down across from me on a matching leather chair and took a drink of her beer. "I bet all of this is making you a bit nervous, huh?"

"Does it show?"

"Oh, not really. I'd say you're handling it very well."

"I'm sort of spinning. I really don't know how to feel."

"Well, maybe in a few days it will come to you. Jeremiah is sure happy that you're here."

"I gathered that."

"I don't believe this has really hit him either."

"What do you mean?"

"He and Jettie were as close as two brothers could get. They did everything together."

"So how long have you and Jeremiah been married?"

She smiled. "Almost thirty years."

"Then you must have known my mom."

"Oh, yes. I knew Bonnie. And I used to hold you when you was just a little thing."

"You did?"

She nodded and her dark brown eyes studied me intently. "You sure look a lot like him."

"Like who?"

"Jettie. You have his sandy hair and his nose. But he had green eyes. You got those brown eyes from your ma."

"I've never seen him so I wouldn't know."

"Not even a picture?"

"No."

"My God, then get your tail over here!"

She stood and walked over to the mantle and grabbed an eight by ten gold-framed photograph and handed it to me. "That's him on the left. The picture was taken two years ago at the NFR."

"NFR?"

"National Finals Rodeo. We go every year."

I studied the photo closely. He and Jeremiah stood next to each other, both smiling, wearing cowboy hats and western shirts. Jeremiah looked the same as he did now. And Jodie was right. With the exception of the eye color I looked a lot like him. But there was a ruggedness about him that also drew a distinct difference between us.

"Was he a good man?" I asked, still looking at him in the photo.

"Sure, everybody loved Jettie. He was like a celebrity around here. And we were all just sure he was going to make us famous. Especially Jeremiah."

"What about my mom?"

"What about her?"

"Did she like him being popular?"

"Not really. Bonnie didn't care much for the rodeo."

"So what actually happened between them?"

"Nobody knows that but your ma. We all have our opinions, but they'd just be gossip and wouldn't do you a bit of good."

"Did you like her?"

"Now Trevor, what kind of question is that?"

"Honestly. I'd like to know what people thought about her."

"I understand, but it would be very disrespectful for me to say anything bad about your ma."

"So you didn't like her."

She slapped me lightly on my arm. "I didn't say that!"

"Look, Jodie, I love my mom. And nothing you or anyone said would ever change that. I don't want gossip, I just want to know your honest feelings."

Her face seemed to tighten up, and I felt as if I was asking her to take a lock off a box of memories she'd rather not open. She looked back up at the mantle and gazed at the many photographs. "I wouldn't know where to start."

"When did you first meet my mom?"

She turned to me and laughed. "How about grade school?"

"You knew her as a child?"

"We went to a little country school between here and Sallisaw. Your Grandpa and Grandma and my folks, and Jeremiah and your daddy's folks were all close friends."

"Wow."

"Even as a young girl, your mom was one of those that always had to be the center of attention or she wasn't happy. She didn't care what other people wanted; all she cared about was whether or not she got what she wanted. She was that way from day one and never changed."

"So did you like her?"

"I liked her, Trevor, but with her personality it was hard to get close to her. It didn't matter what anyone said, when Bonnie wanted something, it was either her way or no way.

"Rodeo was all Jettie ever wanted to do but she fought it like it was some sort of sickness. After you were born, Jettie was offered a job at a factory over in Sallisaw. Driving a forklift and it paid ten dollars an hour. Good money back then. It would have required him to work weekends so he wouldn't have been able to participate in rodeo events. It was when he turned down that job that your mom took you and left."

"Do you think she loved Jettie?"

"Possibly, in her own way."

"What do you mean?"

"Well, haven't you ever been in love?"

This was a weird question, one I wasn't prepared for. "I don't really know."

"If you had, you'd know. It's like Jeremiah and I. When we fell in love there was no greater feeling. But then there comes the part when you have to share your lives. For the most part it's give and take—understanding for that person's needs. That's a level that your mom and Jettie never reached."

"So you're saying that Jettie needed the rodeo to be a complete person, and mom didn't love him enough to let him have it?"

"Sort of. I think she just loved herself more."

This all made sense. All my life Mom pursued men that she could control, and she wanted them to have money so she could maintain a certain image she had committed herself to. When the men would come forward, they'd flaunt their riches, but when it came to getting serious, they'd jump back and eventually clear out, not willing to succumb to Mom's desired reign.

Regardless of my understanding of Mom, from Jettie's point of view this was all difficult for me to understand. I didn't know what it was like to feel such a loss, to have a son, or to love a woman that couldn't provide me with all my needs. This made me think about Amber, and how little we ever shared in regard to intimacy. If she said goodbye to me tomorrow, I wouldn't be upset if she had a good reason for it. And Amber didn't do anything unless she had a good reason.

I handed the picture back to Jodie and she put it back in its place on the mantle. I looked over the many other photographs crowded together, some professional portraits, others snap shots. I noticed one in particular, of Jettie with a young dark-complected woman. She stood next to him smiling as he held a gold oval belt buckle and posed for the picture.

"Who is that?" I said, pointing at the young woman.

"Bella Sonoma. She was your dad's girlfriend the past few years."

"She's pretty. And she looks a lot younger."

"Yeah, she's a looker. Not much older than you, I think."

"Wow, that's interesting."

"Yeah, but she wanted more than Jettie was able to give. I don't think he ever quit loving your mom, and Bella kept trying to take that away."

"Really? Why wouldn't he ever let it go?"

"There's just some things that people can't explain. I'm not sure Jettie even knew. And Bella did everything she could to try and change him."

"Like what?"

"Spoiled him rotten, for one thing. She'd clean his house, cook for him, travel with him to the rodeos and pamper him like a baby. The point was, he never asked for any of it."

"I bet she's taking his death pretty hard."

"She was there at the hospital when they pronounced him dead. She ran from the room and no one has seen her since. She didn't even come to the visitation last night."

I studied the picture closer, the way they smiled, the way he held the buckle up in front of him, and the way she held his arm as he stood for the picture. Her love for him was evident, as was his resistance.

"Does she live around here?" I asked.

"She used to live somewhere down around the Choctaw Nations. The preacher over at the church went looking for her but never found her."

"I'd like to meet her."

"We'll see what we can do. I'm sure she'd be interested in meeting you, too."

SEVEN

I sat with the family in a section of reserved pews normally occupied by the church choir, away from the main pews and to the side of the lectern. Of the three rows that made up the segregated section, we only utilized the front two. Jeremiah had insisted I sit with him and Jodie in the front row, and that Grandpa and Grandma sit behind us. I didn't argue, and neither did my grandparents, though I did feel a bit uncomfortable as people came into the sanctuary and gazed up at me with curiosity.

By the time the funeral started, the small sanctuary of the Methodist church completely filled, with a few people standing at the back. Besides Grandpa, I was one of the only men wearing a suit. Jeremiah wore jeans and a western shirt, the bolo tie he kept in the glove box of his GMC, and a tan corduroy sports jacket with suede patches on the elbows that Jodie made him wear. There were a few other men who wore neckties, but very few, and none I could see who wore a suit jacket of any kind. A man who stood in the back wore blue bib overalls and held a John Deere cap in his hands. But most of the women wore dresses of various styles and colors. Grandma wore the same light blue dress she wore at my graduation, and Jodie wore a half-sleeved, knee length navy blue dress that fit loosely over her slender figure.

Organ music began to play—a soft and dismal tune I didn't recognize. The double doors at the front of the sanctuary swung open, and eventually two men came through the doorway wheeling a silvery-blue metallic looking casket. They wheeled it down the center isle, and when they reached the front of the sanctuary they turned the casket sideways, parallel to the front pews and just below the pulpit. A large spray of red, pink and white flowers lay draped over the center of the casket, and one of the men placed a framed photograph next to the flowers, inducing a few whimpers and sniffles among the crowd. The photo was turned away from me and I couldn't see what it was, but could only assume it was a portrait of "Cowboy Jettie Hodge", for whom we all came to pay our last respects.

A door opened behind the lectern and out walked an older man in a suit and tie bearing the Holy Bible. As soon as he arrived at the podium the organ stopped and he asked everyone to bow their heads and pray. Most everyone did and I followed. The preacher was loud and articulate, and the words he spoke called out to God and His son Jesus to be with us and fill our hearts and minds with strength during this time of tragedy and sorrow. As he continued to pray one of the double doors swung open again and I raised my head slightly and peeked in that direction. A young woman with black hair and sunglasses entered the sanctuary. She wore a sleeveless black dress that stopped just above the knee, a black purse hung over her shoulder, and her arms and legs were tanned like her face. Her sunglasses were also black rimmed, and her hair was pulled tight and when she turned to close the door I saw that it was long and straight and tied in a ponytail. She continued to stand by the doors, crossed her arms and didn't bow her head.

After the prayer the preacher read a scripture from the bible, a verse which he said was in the book of John, and spoke of everlasting life for those who believed in Jesus. Then he read from a prepared speech, which started with the obituary, then a few words of his own about the man he and the community had known, whose spirit now walked with the Lord.

I glanced again at the young woman at the door, who stood almost like a mannequin, but finally dug a tissue out of her purse and dabbed it on her cheeks and under her nose.

Jeremiah nudged me with his elbow then whispered in my ear. "Bella Sonoma."

Ah, yes, I thought. Jettie's, companion. The one that no one could find.

At the cemetery, sitting under a tent while the preacher said his final words, I was able to see the front of the casket, a full view of the colorful spray, and the photograph. Two long red ribbons hung down from the center of the arrangement, with words in silver foil stuck to them. One read "Brother" and another read "Father". And the photograph was a snapshot of Jettie in a cowboy hat, looking back over his shoulder while he carried a saddle. My guess was that they chose the photo because it best represented the man he was.

When the preacher began to read again from the bible, I caught a glimpse of Bella again at the back of the crowd. She stood as she did at the church—still and mysterious behind all black attire. When I noticed her start to walk away, I skipped the reading and went after her. As she was about to get inside a red Ford Mustang, I called her name. She turned and looked at me through her dark, black-rimmed sunglasses, remaining silent as I approached.

"Can I have a minute?"

She continued to stare silently, her sunglasses hiding whatever reaction she had to my presence.

"I'm sorry to bother you, but I'd like to talk to you."

"Who are you?"

Her voice was stout and authoritative.

"I'm Trevor Hodge. I believe you knew my father."

There was a brief silence, and then she removed her sunglasses and stared at me with doleful, bloodshot eyes, as if in awe.

"I hope I'm not upsetting you," I said.

"How did you find out?"

"Jeremiah."

She leaned back against her car, folded the sunglasses and put them in her purse, then retrieved a pack of Marlboro Lights cigarettes and a clear plastic lighter. She lit the cigarette and took a healthy drag, then exhaled thick streams of smoke through her nose.

"So how are you doing?" I asked.

"I smoke a lot."

"Well, for what it's worth, I'm sorry."

She looked at me, as if she were studying my sincerity. "Thank you," she said, a little more at ease.

"I understand you and Jettie were pretty close?"

This made her laugh sarcastically, and then she took another drag from the cigarette. She nodded as she exhaled and looked away toward the cemetery. "Yeah, I guess we were."

"I wish I had more time to talk to you. I'll be going back home this afternoon."

"Where's home?"

"Kansas City."

"So what do you do in Kansas City?"

"Well, I just graduated college. I start work as an accountant tomorrow."

This also made her laugh. "College? Accountant? Maybe that's what it is."

"Excuse me?"

"There's something about you that don't fit. No one would ever know you was Jettie's boy."

"So I'm told."

"What did you want to talk to me about?"

"Well, I never knew him. I just want to know what he was like. That is, if it's not too hard for you to talk about."

She looked toward the crowd then nodded toward the cemetery. "Let's take a walk."

"Sure."

We walked across freshly mowed grass and between rows of headstones. It was almost noon and the air was feeling humid. I loosened my tie and took off my suit coat and carried it over my shoulder.

"So how long did you know him?" I asked.

"We met about six years ago, at the Fort Smith rodeo. I was leading my horse back in the stock area and carrying a bucket of oats when something spooked my horse. It reared and I fell backward and dumped the whole bucket of oats on top of me. I was mad, cussing up a storm, and Jettie was right there when it all happened. He helped me up and while I was complaining about being all dirty, he offered to get more oats and take care of my horse while I cleaned myself up. He was so calm and gentle. I went back to my camper and changed, and when I came back he'd put my horse in a stall, taken off the saddle and put fresh oats in the feeder. Never in my life had a man been so nice to me."

"That seems like a simple favor."

"You don't know my life."

I felt as though we were entering a sensitive area, so I tried not to get off the subject.

"So he was a nice guy?"

She glanced at me, as though disappointed with my next question. "The nicest I ever knew."

"I guess you started dating?"

"If you call it that. We saw each other at all the local rodeos. One time I asked him if he wanted to go riding with me. He did and that's when we exchanged phone numbers."

"You're a rodeo person, too?"

"Barrel racer."

"I see. So you had a lot in common."

"Why do you say that?"

"Well, you both took part in the rodeo."

"Yes, but that's about all we had in common."

"So you two were never serious?"

She stopped walking, dropped the cigarette on the ground and put it out with her shoe, then crossed her arms and gazed out over the cemetery. A single tear ran down her cheek.

"I was, but he wasn't."

"Do you know why?"

She turned her head sharply toward me; her black eyes welled with tears. "Yes, I do. And that's what hurts so much."

She found a used tissue in her purse and dabbed at her eyes.

"It's okay if you can't tell me about it."

"I don't think I can today."

"Fair enough."

"I'm sorry."

"Don't be. Maybe I can call you sometime—at a later date. I'd really like to talk to you again."

Along with her tearful eyes she offered a faint smile, then dug in her purse and pulled out a wrinkled business card and handed it to me.

"I'm a horse trainer on the side. Late evenings are the best time to catch me."

"Great."

"I'm sorry I can't tell you more."

"No, you did great. And I look forward to talking to you again."

She kept looking at me. "You know, I can see the resemblance now." She eventually smiled and shook my hand. "It was nice to meet you."

EIGHT

hen the burial service was over Jodie gave me a
rose from the spray along with the photograph that
stood on top the casket. She gave me a hug and told
me how glad she was that I came, and to finally
meet me after all these years. Jeremiah shook my hand firmly.
His eyes were glassy, but for the most part any emotions he had
he kept to himself.

"Nephew, you being here means a lot."

"I'm glad I came."

"I see that you got to meet Bella."

"Yes, I did."

"How is she holding up?"

"I can tell it's hard for her."

"That's understandable."

We walked out into the crowd and Jeremiah introduced me to
several people. Most were friends and fans from the community,
some associates from the world of rodeo, all offering their
sympathy. One man in particular, who wore a gray felt cowboy
hat and a long-sleeved white western shirt and bolo tie, seemed
like an interesting character.

"This is Denny Rose," Jeremiah said, "a rodeo announcer who lives up in Checotah. He and Jettie were friends for years."

Denny shook my hand with a firm grip and spoke in a vibrant, baritone voice. "Yes, sir," he said. "I thought a lot of your old man. One of the best bull riders I ever laid eyes on."

"Pleased to meet you."

"Likewise, son. If you're ever down this way again, look me up and we'll have a cup of coffee, or maybe something a little stronger." He chuckled and patted my arm with his other hand.

"I'd like that."

"Any time, son."

After sharing a bottle with Jeremiah, I quickly wondered if I'd made a mistake agreeing to drink liquor with this man.

Another man approached and shook Jeremiah's hand. His lower jaw quivered and his eyes were red. He was a lanky older man with a wrinkled face and steel gray hair, wearing a short-sleeved plaid western shirt and blue jeans.

"You doing all right?" he said to Jeremiah.

"It'll take a while. How about you?"

"I'm gonna miss that old rip."

"Me, too."

Jeremiah turned to me. "Trevor, this is Buddy Wells. He used to be a rodeo clown and was one of Jettie's best pals."

We shook hands. "Nice to meet you."

"Buddy," Jeremiah said, "This is Jettie's boy."

The old man found a smile beneath all his sorrow. "I'll be damned. Jettie's boy?"

"That's what they tell me," I said.

"I've sure heard a lot about you," Buddy said.

"You have?"

"Man oh man. Come and see me some time. I'll show you Jettie's favorite fishin' hole."

"That would be fun."

He turned and walked away, shaking hands with several people as he made his way through the crowd.

What a day, I thought. Jettie Hodge, the nicest man Bella ever knew. The best bull rider Denny Rose ever saw. And me, Jettie's boy, who Buddy Wells had heard a lot about.

After lunch, Jeremiah and I slipped away from the post-funeral gathering at his house and drove to a law office on Spiro's Main Street. The attorney invited us in to his office—a plush and stylish room, with the vintage remains of natural oak woodwork stripped and refinished, and on every wall, burgundy and gray velvet flocked wallpaper above wainscoting that matched the trim. We sat near his desk in overstuffed black leather chairs. A matching black leather sofa resided against a wall across from us.

The door to the office opened and the attorney invited the visitor in. "Come on in, Bella."

She was as surprised to see me as I was her, and from the subtle look on Jeremiah's face, I assumed he expected to see her.

I stood to greet her and Jeremiah followed.

"Hi," I said.

"Hi," she said shyly to both of us then looked away.

She sat in the center of the sofa, crossed her legs and arms. She had changed into blue jeans and a red sleeveless shirt, with a belt studded with conchos around her waist and laced boots on her feet. She watched the attorney shuffle papers around on his desk.

"You mind if I smoke, Larry?" she asked.

He handed her an ashtray from his desktop and she quickly lit up. In a matter of seconds a large cloud of white smoke hovered above her and scented the room.

"Let's get started," Larry said.

The executor's duty, to contact all the inheritors and read and execute the will. The situation made me very nervous, to sit among two people who were closest to Jettie and know that my name is somewhere in that will—the name of a person that neither of them, nor Jettie, ever knew.

Larry read through all the legal jargon, and before long got to the meat of the will. Having studied finance, it all sounded very interesting to me, and I was surprised to learn that Jettie was an investor. In the early eighties he had put some money into stock, a couple thousand, and left it all to me. He also left me his house, a tiny three-room shack on the outskirts of Spiro, including all its contents, which I assumed was furniture and various household items. He also owned a piece of Jeremiah's ranch, some livestock which consisted of a few cattle and horses, a Massy Ferguson tractor, and a 1971 Ford pickup, all which he left to me. Plus, the remains of his bank account, a grand total of $6,132.56. I was dumbfounded.

Larry looked at me and smiled. "Trevor, I'm sure this all comes to a great surprise to you."

"I don't know what to say."

I looked at Jeremiah, who smiled back at me.

"This is what Jettie wanted," Jeremiah said.

"That's right," Larry said. "Your father came to me several years ago and we put together this will. Every so often he'd update it, and that's why Bella is here."

I looked over at her. She put out the cigarette in the ashtray and began to cry.

Larry continued. "Trevor, about three years ago Jettie came to me and added Bella to this will. He said to divide everything he had between you and her. He also said to make sure she was taken care of."

I looked at Bella again, who by her tears was obviously having a tough time hearing all this. I looked back at Larry.

"I can understand Bella, but why me?"

"I can't really explain that," Larry said. "But for one thing, you are Jettie's son, and to me that makes a lot of sense."

"But we never knew each other. He may not have even liked me."

Jeremiah laughed and put a hand on my shoulder. "That's not the point, Trevor. He never got to be a father to you and this was his way of making it up to you."

I didn't know what else to say. Two days ago I was a college graduate about to enter the working world to pay off all my student loans and the remaining balance of the debt on my 1997 Honda Accord. Now I'm an heir to a cowboy's fortune—a small balance of a bank account, a few shares of stock, an interest in a ranching operation, and to make sure half of all of it went to a grieving girlfriend.

Larry opened up another folder on his desk. "There's something that will also come to a bit of a surprise."

"Oh, more surprises?" I said laughingly.

"That stock that Jettie bought back in the eighties, it was five hundred shares of Wal-Mart stock. I've been watching that stock for Jettie and the whole time he knew what it was worth, but left it alone."

All of the sudden I felt a rush of blood flow through the main arteries of my neck and into my head, making me feel hot and near faint. My college class had performed a case study on Wal-Mart a couple of years ago, and five hundred shares of stock had to be worth a bundle of cash.

I held my breath as Larry continued.

"Trevor, when Jettie stopped buying that stock it was twenty-eight dollars a share … "

A quick calculation in my head came up with $14,000. But then there were dividends, price increases, and splits!

"After twelve years," Larry said, "five two-for-one splits, and dividend payments, and yesterday that stock closed at 56.7/8." He smiled, "Are you doing the math, son?"

I was, and so far, not knowing the dividend payments, I came up with sixteen thousand shares, and at fifty-six dollars was somewhere in the vicinity of—oh, man—$900,000!

He continued. "Trevor, that little portfolio is now worth over 1.2 million dollars."

I let out a large breath and sunk into my chair. Bella cried into her hands and Jeremiah laughed out loud and put his arm around me.

I felt numb, but suddenly pieces of the puzzle were starting to fit. Now I knew why Jeremiah contacted me. If I didn't come to the funeral, at least he knew where I was. He knew all about the will and he wanted to make sure Jettie got his wish.

Then there was Bella. A woman who loved Jettie, but he couldn't give her the kind of love she wanted in return. This was the only way he could give it back to her. I was amazed at how suddenly we had so much in common.

NINE

Jeremiah handed me a ring of keys and pointed a hand toward Jettie's former home. It was the smallest house I had ever seen; rectangular shaped with white, weathered siding. The front door stood behind a single cement step, and centered between two windows. A box-shaped air conditioner hung outside the window on the right, and to the same side of the house was a matching garage just big enough for one vehicle, with hinged double doors on the end. I looked at Bella, whose eyes still bore the remnants of drying tears.

Jeremiah said, "I better let you two talk things over." In his typical bowlegged style, he walked to his GMC, got in and drove away.

Bella and I went inside the house. It was hotter inside than out, and the air seemed stale and humid. The only light came from a window covered with sheer white curtains. Bella quickly opened one of the windows and turned on a white metal ceiling fan.

The front room was barely big enough for the old green davenport that stretched along the inside wall. One of the legs was missing, with two faded and cobwebby J.C. Penney catalogs in its place. Behind the davenport and on the wall hung a wide wooden-framed painting of a red-orange desert butte. A gold tension rod stretched from floor to ceiling beside it, and hanging near the top of the rod were three cone-shaped lamps that pointed in different directions. Across from the davenport, rabbit ear antennas sprouted from the top of a black Sony TV, and next to the TV was the window that held the air conditioner. Under it all was a hardwood floor, and an oval rug covered most of the area between the davenport and TV.

Out of the front room a short hallway led to a kitchen, a bathroom, and a single bedroom. The kitchen smelled of grease and stale propane gas, and consisted of a single row of varnished plywood cabinets with a laminated countertop, a four-burner gas range, a refrigerator with a rounded top that looked ancient and too big for the room, and a double white porcelain sink mounted in the countertop and below a small window that looked out into the back yard.

The bathroom wasn't much bigger than a closet, with just enough room for the rusty white toilet, a single washbasin that hung on the wall below a cracked mirrored cabinet, and a bathtub with legs that looked like eagle claws.

Inside the bedroom was a full-size wrought iron bed with unmade bedclothes, wadded up and hanging to the floor. A walnut wardrobe stood at the end of the bed with its doors hanging open. Inside several western shirts hung on wire hangers, and below the shirts, a shelf and two drawers that expanded the width of the wardrobe. On top of the wardrobe, several straw and felt cowboy hats stacked atop one another. But the most interesting of all were a series of shelves that hung on one wall of the room and completely filled with trophies and photographs from rodeo events. I walked along and studied several of them, pulled one of the trophies off and, with my thumb, wiped the dust off the engraved brass plate. It read "Second Place, 1985 Staked Plains Rodeo". Then I studied the gold statuette; a man in a cowboy hat with one arm in the air, riding a bull with its front feet on the ground and its back feet kicked high in the air.

"Those are nothing," Bella said, standing in the bedroom doorway with her arms crossed. She walked over to the wardrobe and opened up a drawer and pulled out a black shoebox. After she removed the lid I looked inside at several items wrapped in white tissue paper.

"What's in here?" I asked.

"Buckles."

"I don't understand."

"Come sit down." She sat on the bed and I sat beside her. She took one of the tissue-wrapped bundles out of the box, removed the tissue and handed the buckle to me. It was shiny with gold banners zigzagging on a silver background, the outside border simulated a golden rope, and engraved on the banners were "1988 Mesquite Championship Rodeo", "Bull Rider" and "1st Place".

"He was very proud of these," Bella said.

"I can see why. They're beautiful."

She pulled another buckle out of the box and removed the tissue. "He won this one for qualifying for the 1994 Bud Light Cup tour."

"Qualifying?"

"Only the top forty-five riders every year can qualify for the tour."

"Top forty-five, in Oklahoma?"

"No, in the world."

I studied the buckle again. "Wow."

She stood from the bed and walked over to the shelves. She took down a photo and brought it to me. It appeared to be Jettie when he was younger, standing in front of a metal gate next to another cowboy, and a black ink autograph was scribbled across the photo."

"Who's this?"

"That's Jettie with Don Gay, famous bull rider and old Rodeo buddy who's now a famous TV announcer."

"No kidding?"

She grabbed another photo and brought it to me. "This is one of his favorites, with Casey Tibbs."

The photo was black and white; the cowboy squatted on one knee with his arm around a little boy wearing a cowboy hat.

"The little boy, is that Jettie?" I asked.

"Cute, huh."

"Who is Casey Tibbs?"

"Jettie's boyhood hero. He holds the world record for the most Saddle Bronc titles."

This was all so interesting. A world I had never been exposed to, but the man that gave me life knew it like nothing else.

"Explain something to me," I said, looking around the room. "If he was so good, why did he live this way?"

"For the most part, rodeo is an expensive career. Some cowboys don't break even after the travel expenses and entry fees are paid. Jettie did all right, his best year he cleared about sixty thousand. But he put most of that back into the ranch. He cared less for material things."

"Makes sense. He owned over a million dollars worth of stock and never cashed it in."

This comment sparked a bit of emotion within Bella and tears filled her eyes.

"Are you okay?" I asked.

She wiped at her tears and gazed up at the pictures and trophies. "I want you to know that I knew nothing about the money."

"Of course you didn't."

"I wouldn't want you to think I was some kind of gold digger or something."

I stood from the bed. "Jettie wanted you to have it, so apparently you deserved it."

She cried harder and came to me and wrapped her arms around my waist. She laid her head against my chest and wept. I was slow to return the comfort she desired, but when I finally held her it was firm and strangely perfect.

"I miss him so much," she said.

"I'm sure you do."

She eventually let loose of me, took a deep breath and wiped her cheeks with the palms of her hands. "I'm sorry."

"Don't be."

"Why don't we go outside?"

"Sure."

We walked out the back door and into the yard. Next to the door was a rusty barbecue grill and two foldable lawn chairs. We walked around to the garage and opened the double doors. The daylight exposed the tailgate of the 1971 Ford Pickup mentioned in the will. It was two toned—turquoise on bottom and white on top, with a rectangular bale of hay in the back.

"Well, how do we divide the truck?" I asked.

She laughed. "You can have that old bucket of bolts. I'll stick with my Mustang."

I walked further into the garage; the dirt floor dispelled dampness and made the air smell musty. I opened the driver side door and gazed inside. The dash was cracked badly in several places and the seat was torn in the driver area, exposing the beige stuffing and iron seat springs. Before stepping inside, I instinctively looked down below the door and checked for cattle manure. I sat in front of the steering wheel, found a square-ended Ford key, put it in the ignition and started the engine, which roared and sputtered. I pressed the gas pedal and smoothed it out, and when I let off, the exhaust pipes rapped and popped.

I laughed to myself, thinking that this was Jettie's only transportation and the guy could have afforded anything he wanted. I shut it off and climbed out. Bella still stood at the opening of the garage.

"Neat old truck, huh?" she said.

"Yeah, very neat," I said sarcastically.

"That was another one of Jettie's pride and joys."

"This old truck?"

"His father bought it new when Jettie was in high school, and he later gave it to him. It's part of the family."

"I see."

I shut the garage doors and we walked to the front step of the house, where we sat next to each other and stared out into the yard.

"So what do we do now?" I asked.

"Larry said he'd handle the details for us. Now, I guess we have to try and get back to our normal routines."

"Yeah, you're right."

"So what are you going to do?"

"Go back to Kansas City. Start my job."

"Do you think you'll like being an accountant?"

"I hope so. It's all I know."

"You could do like my mother did."

"What's that?"

"She's a beautician, and once she developed a clientele, she opened up her own beauty parlor."

"Are you saying I should open up my own accounting office?"

"Why not? You got the money now to do it."

"Yeah, I guess I do."

The thought of having over a half-million dollars in net worth still hadn't quite soaked in. And to make it seem right, I had to keep telling myself the same thing I told Bella, that it was what Jettie wanted. Suddenly I wondered how I would explain my sudden riches to Mom. How ironic, I thought, that she would leave her husband in search of a life of vanity and wealth, and for him to one day become a millionaire. Telling her would not be easy, and the more I thought about it, probably not a very good idea at all.

TEN

efore going back to Kansas City I had one last bit of detail to go over with Jeremiah, which involved Jettie's interest in the ranch. It was a small interest, about ten percent, but with an approximate net value of $60,000, which I had to split with Bella, of course. This included a percentage of the land, livestock, farm equipment, several stock trailers and other vehicles, the house and buildings, and even Jeremiah's GMC. He said he'd be willing to buy me out or I could keep the interest, whichever I preferred. I had no idea what to do at the time so I decided to think about it.

The drive back to Kansas City took better than six hours. Along the way, we stopped in Bentonville, Arkansas, the official headquarters of Wal-Mart Stores, Incorporated, and toured the Wal-Mart Visitor's Center. Grandpa wondered why I had a sudden interest in Wal-Mart and I told him about studying the company in college, and that I was very impressed with their financial success. Well, I wasn't lying.

Like I told Jeremiah and Bella, I didn't want anyone knowing about the inheritance—especially Mom. And this included Grandpa, because he'd tell Grandma, and then Grandma would tell Mom. It was an ingrained system, guaranteed to work every time. So Jeremiah agreed that it was our little secret.

*   *   *

My first day on the job was not near as exciting as I once had expected. I wore my favorite suit as planned, and my cubicle was complete with all the hardware I had dreamed of. A state of the art desktop computer with all the software one could use, Internet access to obtain investment information, a professional ten-key calculator, and a free pass to the office supply closet.

I placed a picture of Mom and I at the graduation on the desk of my cubicle, one that she had developed and framed specifically for my new office. Also from the same roll of film, I stuck an unframed photo of Amber and I on the tacking strip that ran across the cubicle wall. And next to the photo of my mom and I, I stood the picture of Jettie that Jodie gave me at the funeral.

Seeing the photo again made me smile and think of the wonderful time I had meeting my lost family. I still didn't quite know what to think of the inheritance. For some reason I didn't feel like I deserved it, even though Jeremiah felt otherwise, and it was Jettie's wish. You don't have to be an accountant to appreciate a sudden net worth of almost $700,000. But I've always been the type to want to earn what I have, and I never expected things to be handed to me on a silver platter. Mom, however, was a different story. Wealth and status were very important to her, and she didn't care how she obtained it. I always knew this about her, but for some reason it never really bothered me until now. I guess it was because for so long she was all that I had.

My first week on the job was almost painless, spending most of my time in orientation and training courses. Rather than concentrating on learning the specifics of the Bennett and Dobbs clientele base, quite often I found myself drifting away, thinking about rodeo buckles, bucking bulls, shots of corn whiskey, a dog named Jezebel, a little white house, an old Ford pickup, Jeremiah's comforting smile, and the tears of Bella Sonoma. But my second week got worse. I was not the Magna cum laude that

Bennett and Dobbs had hired. I kept making mistakes with my ten-key, entering the wrong numbers on client spreadsheets, and filing stuff in the wrong place. My cubicle became disorderly, and at one point I became so angry that I violently tore the printout tape off the calculator and slammed my fist on the keypad. I ran my fingers through my hair and cursed as the calculator spit out a tape full of useless numbers.

An older woman in a neighboring cubicle stood and peeked over at me.

"Mind your own damned business!" I yelled.

She disappeared quickly.

I rested my elbows on my desk and hid my face with my hands. I couldn't understand what was happening to me. I felt lost and deprived, as if I starved for something and would lose my mind if I didn't satisfy this hunger.

I leaned back in my chair and let out a deep breath. I looked closely at the picture of Mom and me, how happy we seemed, but then I remembered who showed up during that photograph.

I looked at Jettie's picture. In the short time I had learned about him I became peculiarly attracted to that cowboy image, and the history of the man that everyone loved.

I couldn't take anymore and decided to go for a walk downtown. I grabbed my suit coat off a hanger in the cubicle and walked to the elevator. From our office on the eighth floor I went to ground level, and then walked down Tenth Street, across Baltimore Avenue and eventually to Main. I sat down on a bench in an outside food court near the Town Pavilion, a thirty story skyscraper that claimed the status of Kansas City's newest and tallest building.

I peered up at the skyline of the buildings, observed the many panes of mirrored glass that reflected the sunlight, the blue sky, and the neighboring buildings. This scene made me reflect back to the ranch, and realize how the setting was so opposite. Suddenly I longed again to see the cattle grazing in the pasture, hear the screeching and singing of prairie birds, smell the fragrance of fresh cut hay, feel the wind of the plains blow through my hair, and amazingly the scorching taste of Jeremiah's whisky.

I leaned over and put my elbows on my knees when I felt something crinkle in my inside coat pocket. I reached inside and pulled out an envelope, finding the letter that Jeremiah gave me. I remembered that I put the letter in my inside pocket the day of the funeral, thinking I would read it that day. But I got caught up in all that was happening with Bella and the inheritance and forgot all about it.

I slid my index finger inside the small opening under the flap on the back of the envelope and tore it open. The letter was written on a small piece of stationery, similar to a page from a steno pad, and in blue cursive ink. Though the handwriting was not good, it was legible.

January 17, 1978

Dear Bonnie,

You know I'm not much with words, so these letters are hard for me to write. All I know to say is that I miss you and my boy. It's been two months now since you left, and the place is empty without the two of you here. I can't even think about my work that needs done, not even the rodeo season coming up. All I can think about is you and the baby. This is your home and you are welcome back anytime. I need you Bonnie and I need my little one. It just ain't right living without my family. Please come home.

All my love,
Jettie

It all seemed so simple and familiar. A man who felt lost and deprived. And those last three words, "Please come home," stayed with me the rest of the day, while I worked out at the fitness center, when I slept at night, and for the rest of the week.

Thursday night I dreamed again about the clowns approaching me in my cubicle. Now I recognized the trophy, the photograph, and more of the people who cheered and applauded. There was Bella, Denny Rose, and behind his makeup I recognized Buddy Wells. But I couldn't figure out the ovation. What did I do to deserve it? What did I do to deserve anything?

Friday morning I went to my cubicle as usual. Friday's were casual days so I dressed in cotton khaki slacks and a knit polo shirt. I had no more than turned on my computer when Kyle Bennett entered my cubicle.

"Good morning, Trevor."

"Good morning."

"Can I have a minute?"

"Sure."

"Great. Come to my office."

I followed him to a walled-in office at the end of the cubicle section. He told me to have a seat and pointed at a pair of hunter green, overstuffed chairs in front of his desk, and then he closed the door behind us. He sat in his high-backed black leather chair and crossed his legs. He also wore casual attire similar to mine.

"I've been wanting to visit with you, Trevor. You've been here a couple of weeks, and like all new people, I like to touch base and see how things are going."

"Things are going pretty well." I lied.

"Well, it's been brought to my attention that things haven't been going too well for you."

I wasn't surprised to hear this. "No, actually, I've not been myself lately."

"Well, it's understandable, losing your father and all."

"Yeah, it's been hard."

"You know, I did some checking, and through certain sources I learned that you never knew your father."

I *was* surprised to hear this. "Sources?"

He rested his right elbow on the chair armrest, raised his hand and twirled an ink pen around his fingers. He raised his eyebrows and gazed at me condescendingly. "You know, I expected a lot better from you, Trevor. The Dean had nothing but good things to say about you."

"So do you think the Dean was lying?"

"I don't know, was he?"

Suddenly Kyle reminded me of Walter, AKA Penis Head. "Well," I said, "I'll just be frank with you, Mr. Bennett. My personal life is none of your business."

I surprised myself with this one, and I could tell by the irritated look on his face that he didn't appreciate the response.

"Interesting attitude," he said. "The Dean never mentioned that."

I studied his antagonizing glare and felt an instant distaste for him, the firm, and the job. I no longer felt a sense of challenge or accomplishment. There was no evidence of prestige that I had expected from a metropolitan accounting firm. And the camaraderie and respect between coworkers, especially Kyle Bennett, was nonexistent. At once I felt compelled to escape this feeling of emotional bondage, to let loose of everything that kept me from experiencing the new fire that burned inside my head and my heart.

I stood from the chair and leaned forward, and he appeared to stop breathing as I rested my hands on his desk. "You know something else the Dean didn't tell you about me?"

He didn't answer, but returned a glare as if we were in a pistol duel.

I continued. "I'm sure the Dean didn't tell you that I don't waste my time dealing with small people."

Then I pointed a finger at him. "And let me tell you something else! I didn't know my father very well, but I do know one thing about him. He had more heart than you'll ever have. Too much to sit in some high-backed chair and throw his weight around, insulting people in the process. Kyle, you need to get a life. And while you're out finding it, I'll be out living mine."

I'm sure he felt a cool breeze as I slammed the door on my way out, but it could not have been as fresh as the air in my lungs as I grabbed my personals and left Bennett and Dobbs for good.

ELEVEN

here was something strangely satisfying about packing
everything I owned inside my Honda Accord and
driving off into the countryside. Besides the Nike T-
shirt, khaki shorts, and Doc Martin sandals I had on, I
stuffed nearly all my clothing in three duffel bags and stacked
them in the back seat. The few items on wire hangers, which
consisted only of four button-up shirts, I hung on a travel hook
behind the driver's seat. I decided to leave the suits and
accessories, since I had already experienced enough about Spiro
to know that even in church the most casual attire was
acceptable. And besides a few other miscellaneous items I felt I
couldn't live without, like books and photographs, I abandoned
the rest for Mom to deal with.

Breaking the news to her wasn't easy, and of course,
according to her I was making one of the biggest mistakes of my
life. Under different circumstances, having quit my job, I think
she would have kicked me out of the house. But since I was
leaving on my own initiative, everything was beyond her control
and I sensed that this bothered her most. She asked me about
money, wondering how I'd survive. I told her not to worry, that
something would eventually work out. For God's sake, if she
only knew. I'd never felt such pity for my mother before and it

was not a good feeling, so the best I could do was give her a hug, tell her I loved her, and get on my way.

On my way out of town I stopped at Amber's apartment. My initial approach to her came with guilt, because for some reason I made it sound as if I was breaking up with her. Her response came with a tone of laughter, reminding me that we had never made a commitment to each other so there was nothing to break off. This is what I liked about her. I told her that she was a great friend, that I valued my relationship with her and I didn't want any hard feelings. She hugged me and told me that I obviously had something very important going on or I wouldn't be doing it. Her support was priceless.

I arrived in Spiro a little before noon on Saturday, and as I crossed the bridge over Spiro Beach, I noticed some activity at the rodeo arena. There were only three vehicles in the parking lot: two pickups, one a yellow Chevy, the other a black Dodge connected to a lengthy cage-like trailer of the same color, and a red Ford Mustang. Curious, I drove into the parking lot and parked beside the Mustang then looked out into the arena. I hardly recognized Bella under the shade of her straw cowboy hat, but the Ford Mustang convinced me it was her.

I got out of my car and leaned over the fence. Bella ran the horse at full stride, turned it around a large blue barrel, then another, then slapped each side of the animal's rump with what looked like a strap of leather and galloped toward the end of the arena. She ran toward a man who also wore a straw cowboy hat and held a stopwatch. He clicked the stopwatch as she ran by.

"Sixteen and ninety-two!" He yelled.

After she stopped and dismounted from the horse a man in a faded red cap took the reins from her, looked my way and nodded. She looked at me, and without looking away said something to him then walked to me.

Besides the cowboy hat, she wore dark blue skintight jeans, a white long-sleeved western shirt and lace-up boots. She removed a pair of tawny looking leather gloves from her hands and slapped them against her thigh, emitting a small cloud of dust.

"So is that a good score?" I said, along with a smile.

"Not if I'm going to take money home," she said in a frustrated tone, then glanced over her shoulder into the arena. "And in this oval there's no pressure of competition. No crowd or announcer to distract you."

"I see."

She looked back at me and offered what seemed to be a fabricated smile. "So how's the new job?"

"Didn't work out."

"Oh—sorry to hear that."

"Don't be."

"So what brings you back here?"

"I decided to take a little summer vacation."

"In Spiro?"

"Why not?"

"I'm sure there's more to do in Kansas City."

"Not in my mind."

"So what are your plans?"

"Oh, one day at a time."

Now her smile seemed genuine. "I never thought of you as a guy without a plan."

"That is my plan."

"What is?"

"One day at a time."

This made her laugh. "Whatever."

I enjoyed her laughter, and different than before, there was something enchanting about the way she looked. Not just in her clothes, which emphasized the trim contour of her hips and breasts, but in her natural beauty, distinct by the color of her skin, her long black hair, pushed behind her ears and held in place by her hat, and the brown irises of her eyes that seemed to hold me in submission.

"Have you had lunch?" I asked.

"No, are you inviting me?"

"Now you have me all figured out."

*   *   *

We settled in a booth at Barny's, a small café and one of the few businesses still in operation on Spiro's Main Street. But despite the image of economic despair, Barny's seemed to be thriving. The café was long and narrow, bowling alley shaped, with a bar and several bar stools lining one side, a single isle of chrome legged tables and chairs in the center, and a row of dark green vinyl booths lined the other side. Like the booths, the cushions on the chairs and barstools were covered in dark green vinyl and nearly all occupied by hungry, cigarette-smoking customers. Framed photographs crowded the walls, several of various seasons of little league baseball teams, all wearing shirts with Barny's name screen printed on the front. And I wasn't surprised to see several rodeo pictures. I looked closely at one, recognizing Jettie standing next to a man in a black Barny's T-shirt and straw cowboy hat. The photo was inscribed, "To Barny, Best Wishes, Jettie Hodge, Old Fort Days Rodeo, May 29, 1992."

A young, pregnant waitress brought us each a clear glass of ice water and silverware rolled in a white paper napkin. She greeted Bella by name and asked her how she was holding up.

"It'll be a while," she said, then nodded at me. "Tanya, did you know Jettie had a son?"

Tanya's eyes rounded in astonishment as she looked at me.

"Nice to meet you," I said.

She dug an ordering pad out of a pocket on her maternity smock, then smiled gingerly at me. "Oh, hon, don't feel bad."

"About what?" I asked.

"It's okay to be a bastard child. This will be my second and its daddy done gone run off, too."

Bella slapped her arm. "Tanya!"

"It's okay," I said.

"Oh, I'm sorry," Tanya said. "I hope I didn't offend you."

"No, you didn't."

Bella quickly changed the subject and ordered a cheeseburger and fries with a Dr. Pepper and I ordered the same. Tanya scribbled down our order on the pad, then tore the page off and took it to a wide window at the end of the lengthy room and clipped it onto a stainless steel carousel along with several other order slips. A man in a white T-shirt with big hairy forearms grabbed the ticket.

Bella lit a cigarette then gazed at me through the exhale of smoke. "I hope you don't mind my smoking."

"Suit yourself."

"I just started the day after Jettie died. It keeps me calm."

"Hopefully in time you won't need them."

She looked down at the smoldering cigarette lodged between her two fingers, as if she contemplated putting it out, but succumbed to it once again and took another healthy drag.

"So," she said through another vaporous exhale, "you're really going to spend some time in Spiro?"

"That's the plan."

"So what are you going to do?"

"I was hoping to spend some time with Jeremiah, and with you."

From the way her eyes smiled and glanced nervously away, I feared my request scared her.

"Me?"

"But if it's too difficult for you, I understand."

"I won't know until you ask."

"Okay. I want to learn more about Jettie. I want to live like he lived. Meet his friends. Travel the rodeo. Spend the whole summer here if I have to. Whatever it takes, I want to know who my father was."

"You're serious."

"I am, but if it's too hard, I'll back off."

"What do you want me to do?"

"Just show me the life."

She nodded and tapped her cigarette into a clear glass ashtray, then studied my hair, my chest, then leaned over and looked under the table.

"Is something wrong?" I asked.

"Nothing that can't be fixed."

"What do you mean?"

"If you're going to hang with me, we've got to get you in the proper attire."

"I have jeans, if that's what you mean."

"What kind of jeans?"

"Levi, Tommy Hilfiger."

She laughed. "Won't work, cowboy."

"They won't?"

"First of all, you got to have some boots. And if you're gonna be a cowboy, you got to wear Wrangler jeans."

"What kind do you wear?"

"Some Wranglers, but mostly Lawman and they're just for ladies."

"So you're saying that all cowboys wear Wrangler jeans?"

"No, not all of them. But most of them do."

"What did Jettie wear?"

"I was afraid you'd ask that. He wore Levi's."

"Then that's what I'm going to wear."

"Oh, no, not another one."

"I want to experience life like he did. And if that means wearing the same kind of jeans, then so be it."

Tanya arrived with our order and laid the check next to me. Our burgers and fries heaped on pieces of wax paper spotted with grease, and tucked inside red, oval-shaped plastic baskets. Our Dr. Peppers nearly overflowed with crushed ice inside tall, white plastic glasses, with straws standing inside the mound of ice. "Can I get you two anything else?" Tanya asked.

Bella shook her head and so did I. But suddenly I decided to ask her for an opinion.

"Tanya?"

"Yes, hon?"

"What kind of jeans do you prefer on a cowboy?"

This prompted a seductive smile. "Them Wranglers look pretty good, but it's hard to beat a cowboy butt in a pair of Levi's."

Bella cried. "Tanya, you are no help!"

We both laughed as Tanya walked away. Bella put out her cigarette in the ashtray, then grabbed a bottle of catsup, patted on the bottom of the bottle and poured a glob into her basket. She handed the bottle to me and I did the same.

"Seriously now," I said. "You surely don't judge a cowboy by the type of jeans he wears?"

"You sound just like your old man."

"I do?"

"So many cowboys would spend themselves broke trying to look good in the saddle, when Jettie probably wore the same clothes for ten years."

"Was he tight?"

"No, just practical."

"From the standpoint of an accountant, I can respect that."

She laughed suddenly. "I remember one time we were in Las Vegas for the National Finals, and we got invited to a party. It was at some well-to-do's fancy ranch out in the desert. I took Jettie to a shop at one of them casino hotels, and I told him I was going to buy him an outfit for the party. He always carried a pair of reading glasses in his shirt pocket, and he had to pull them out to have a second look at the price tag on one of the sports jackets I wanted him to try on."

"Was it expensive?"

"Compared to J.C. Penney, it was outrageous. Jettie whistled and said, 'Ain't no way I'm paying six hundred dollars for something I'll wear once.' But I said he wasn't paying six hundred for it, I was, and to try it on or I was going to the party by myself."

"Did he do it?"

"Oh yes, and I bought it, along with a pair of slacks, a hundred dollar shirt, and a new pair of ostrich skin boots. The whole getup cost over twelve hundred dollars and he looked fabulous."

"That is a lot of money for one outfit."

"Yeah, but you only live once."

"Did he have a good time at the party?"

She laughed again. "He stood stiff as aboard all night, afraid someone was going to step on his boots or spill something on his coat. He was a hoot."

Her smile and laughter quickly faded and her eyes glazed with tears as she dipped a french-fry in catsup and took a bite.

"Are you sure you can do this?" I asked.

She swallowed and tried to cover her sorrow with a smile. "It won't be easy, but for Jettie, and his son, I can't imagine not doing it."

TWELVE

ince the funeral Bella had so graciously cleaned the entire house. It smelled now of pine scented cleaner. The floors and furniture were dusted, the windows clean, and the toilet was now white and free from rusty stains. Even the wardrobe doors were closed properly and the bedclothes made. I remembered how Jodie had said that Bella had spoiled Jettie, and this was likely a good sampling of how she had taken care of him. But a stranger thought, it reminded me of how my mom took care of our home. It was always clean and spotless; in fact I think a person could eat off our floors.

After unpacking all my bags and sharing a few laughs about my city clothes, Bella retrieved a few items of Jettie's clothing, including the expensive outfit she had bought for him in Las Vegas. She opened a dresser drawer and under several pair of faded jeans, located his one pair of Wranglers, unfolded them and held them up for me to see. Unlike the others they were still very dark.

"You know," she said, "you look about the same size." She held them up to my waist.

"What size did he wear?"

She found a tag inside the waistline and read it off. "32 by 34."

"That's exactly my size."

She grinned triumphantly and handed them to me. "Then let's see them on, cowboy!"

She stood as if she were going to watch me take off my shorts, but I kindly asked her for some privacy. She apologized and said she would go to the kitchen and get us a beer. In an odd way, I liked the premonition that she felt so comfortable around me that she could watch me take my clothes off. But I quickly removed any stray thoughts of us getting naked and concentrated on the curiosity at hand.

The jeans were much tighter than I was used to, but they had an interesting feel about them. As if I had just put on some uniquely designed gear that would help me better accomplish whatever it was I was supposed to do. I tucked in my shirt and zipped up the jeans, then found the ostrich skin boots near the base of the wardrobe. They were a bit dusty so I wiped them off with my hand, sat on the edge of the bed and pulled them on, then pushed the cuffs of the jeans down over the tall uppers. When I stood I felt like I had grown six inches in height, and almost felt as if I could see the world from a different perspective.

I pulled down one of the straw hats from the stack on top the wardrobe. It seemed to fit okay, and like the other garments, made me feel as though I had just acquired something special, if not powerful. I looked at myself in a long mirror that hung on the inside of the wardrobe door. I turned and looked over my shoulder at my backside and heard a wolf whistle from the doorway.

"Not bad," Bella said, smiling and holding a longneck beer bottle in each hand.

We spent the rest of the afternoon trying on pieces of Jettie's wardrobe, and I couldn't believe how well everything fit.

"Jettie must have been pretty trim for an older guy," I said.

"He stayed in shape," she said. "He had a constant routine of lifting weights and jogging."

"No kidding? Where did he work out?"

"Right here in this room and out there on the street." She dropped to her knees and pulled several items from under the bed. There was a pair of Adidas running shoes, several cast iron dumbbells of various weights, bars, and a back support belt.

"I'm impressed," I said.

"He had a routine of jogging early every morning and lifting weights when he returned from the run. He was very adamant about staying in shape."

"Did you ever work out with him?"

"No, I belong to a fitness center at the Poteau hospital. I just do aerobics and the treadmill. It keeps me in shape for riding. Do you work out?"

"While I was in college I used the campus fitness center three days a week. My new employer provided me with a discount to a health club of my choice, and I planned to continue, but I hadn't thought about it until now."

"Well maybe you should work out with me?"

I looked down at Jettie's equipment, trying to come up with an answer that wouldn't hurt her feelings. "How about we alternate?"

"What do you mean?"

"Every other day I work out with you at the fitness center, the other days you work out with me, here."

She nodded and smiled. "I can do that."

"Great. But for now, let's have another beer and relax."

She agreed, grabbed us each a fresh beer and we retired to the living room davenport. I was surprised to discover how tired I was, but more so how comfortable the old piece of furniture felt.

"I had fun today," Bella said.

"Me, too."

This was the first I had seen her in such a relaxed state and wondered if it was the first of any time she had experienced such composure since Jettie's death. She spun sideways and folded her leg, placed her foot underneath her other thigh and faced me. "So, you think you can handle living the summer in this old cowboy castle?"

I scanned around the room then smiled back at her. "Sure, why not?"

She returned a tender smile. "You know, even though you are very different from Jettie, you do share that same amazing power of endurance."

"Oh, how's that?'

"I'm just impressed at how you'd pack up and come down here, and expose yourself to a life you know nothing about."

"You're impressed, but I'm terrified."

"Then I was right about that, too."

"How so?"

From the way the radiance in her face seemed to dwindle, I could tell we were entering a sensitive area, and suddenly I was mad at myself for leading her away from her serene state. But I was somewhat relieved to see her come back with a slight smile.

"Well, what you're doing is sweet," she said. "The interest you are showing in Jettie—it's almost as if you're answering his call."

"His call?"

Whatever thoughts were in her head, she had to ponder them a bit, and she turned to face me completely now, with both legs up on the davenport, folded together.

"Next to Jeremiah," she said, "I probably knew Jettie better than anyone. But there was still a huge part of his life that was shut off and pushed away. I don't think he even allowed himself to face it very often."

"Do you have any idea what it was?"

"Oh yes, I'm pretty sure."

"What?"

"It was you."

"Me?"

"Even though he spoke of you only twice, I'm sure it was you. It was when I asked him if he'd ever been married before. I could tell this was something he hated to bring up, but since we were close I think he felt I deserved an answer. So he told me that he had been married once, and that he had a son. He told me her name and your name, and that she left him when you were a baby and took you away."

"Was that it?"

"That time, yes. But one time we were both having a very good time, out at a dance club in Fort Smith. I felt so close to him that night and I wanted to—you know—be with him. But when we got home, he wanted to say goodnight. I was very hurt and I asked him what was wrong with me. He tried to assure me that it had nothing to do with me. We got in a fight and didn't talk to each other for a couple days."

"So what happened?"

"The next time we got together I asked him why he wouldn't get close to me. And that was the second and only other time I heard about you. He said that the last time he made love to a woman, she took the result away, and he couldn't bear to have that happen again."

"That's really strange. I mean, he didn't even know me, and all you wanted was to share some affection."

"That's what I felt at first. So I asked him why he didn't try and find you. He said that it had been too long, and that he didn't think it was fair to you to all the sudden show up and try to be a father to you."

"That would have been weird."

"You see, he was a very unselfish man. And I also think he was scared."

"A man who rides bulls is scared to face his only son?"

"You might say he had a soft side. It's really no different than a man who deep sea dives, or walks along steel girders thirty stories in the air. Bull riding was his profession, and that was it."

Pieces of the puzzle were starting to fit together for me. I understood where she was coming from, and what she meant by "…answering his call". It was like Jeremiah said, Jettie never got to be a father to me and the inheritance was all he was able to give. And me being here, learning about my heritage and the life my father lived, that maybe he hoped I would one day understand why things happened the way they did. I didn't have those answers yet, but it seemed I was on the right track.

As I looked back at her, I wondered how much more she could tell me about Jettie. Then suddenly I realized that I knew very little about her. I knew that she was a barrel racer and a horse trainer, and that she was Jettie's closest companion.

"So tell me about yourself," I said.

She smiled, almost embarrassingly. "What's to tell?"

"I'm sure there's a lot of things. I'd like to know where you live and where you came from. And maybe I'll learn why Jettie cared so much about you."

"How do you know he did?"

"Come on, Bella."

She took a deep breath and reached for her purse on the floor, and pulled out a pack of cigarettes.

"Oh, no," I said. "No smoking."

"What?"

"If this is going to be my house I prefer a smoke free environment."

"You're serious?"

"Really, I just want you to talk to me without the security of a Marlboro between your fingers."

Somewhat defeated, she dropped the pack of cigarettes on the floor and put her hands back in her lap. Then she looked at me and sneered. "And here I thought you were going to be a lot of fun."

"Sorry to disappoint you."

"Why don't we go out? It's too quiet around here. I almost feel like I'm talking to a shrink."

"What do you suggest?"

"I know a place, and I promise I won't smoke, I just need a different atmosphere."

"Ok, let's do it."

My agreement put a healthy smile back on her face, and a spring in her step as she led me to the bedroom and picked out an outfit for me to wear. I was not surprised at the ensemble she laid before me—the Wrangler jeans, straw hat and Ostrich skin boots—and after putting it all together again I somehow knew that I was about to experience the nightlife of eastern Oklahoma.

THIRTEEN

T he hot spot for nightlife in Kansas City was the one and only Westport, an area of south central Kansas City known historically as a trading post for pioneers heading west. But today Westport and its antiquity was party central for the majority of area college students or any over twenty-one drink and dance personality. All the buildings had transformed into bars or dance clubs of some sort, promoting different genres of music and culture. Ernie and I usually started at Kelly's, an Irish pub that was nothing more than a watering hole for patrons to gather and get primed. Then it was off to whatever dance club we desired. One time we went to a club that played country music and offered a wooden platform for line dancing. Neither the music nor the fun were familiar to us, so we left and never went back. But tonight that scene came back to me as Bella and I drove out east of Spiro and down a gravel road, to a joint that seemed to be in the middle of nowhere, with a huge neon sign on the roof that blinked the word "BEER".

Inside this place called "BEER" was a crowd of people in cowboy hats and farm caps, talking loud and laughing over music from a jukebox (a country song I didn't recognize) all inside a gray haze of cigarette and cigar smoke and very dim light, which came mostly from neon lights that hung on the walls throughout the bar and advertised various brands of beer. In one corner two cowboys stood next to a billiard table (which I soon learned was properly termed "pool table") holding cue sticks. A rectangular Busch Beer lamp hung above the table, which in the dim bar made the cowboys seem like a spectacle. And next to them stood a contraption that I could not identify, which looked like a large brown leather suitcase tilted on a pedestal. It sat idle and obscure, and for the life of me, I couldn't imagine a single valid use or purpose for its existence.

Between the contraption and the pool table were two sets of swinging doors, similar to those found in an old-fashioned saloon like seen in a western movie, and above each set of doors were signs, one reading "Cowboys" and the other "Cowgirls".

Bella and I found a vacant table at one end of the room opposite the pool table. We ordered a pitcher of Bud Light and the waitress, a young blonde in a cowboy hat, yellow T-shirt, and cutoff blue denim shorts, brought it to us along with two frosty mugs.

I wasn't a connoisseur of any certain type of music; in fact my taste was pretty broad. I enjoyed everything from modern rock to classic guitar. Some of my favorite music came from local bands in Kansas City, some performing blues or reggae or a modern version of folk music. I had never drawn much of an opinion of country music, but some of it was pretty catchy, like the song that now played on the jukebox, which Bella informed me was *Whose Bed Have Your Boots Been Under* by Shania Twain.

I motioned to Bella that she had a line of beer foam on her upper lip. "Bella, got beer?"

She snickered and wiped it off.

"So, are you a regular here?" I asked.

"Not really. But I do like to come when they have live music."

"You mean people actually perform here?"

"Every Friday night some local band will come in. Sometimes they bring in artists from Arkansas or Texas. They're really pretty good."

"Well, the name of the place is certainly original."

"What do you mean?"

"What better name is there for a place like this than 'BEER'?"

This made her laugh and nearly cough up a gulp of beer, but she managed to get it down without choking. "It's called The Oasis. The light on the main sign is burnt out. The only one working is the 'BEER' sign."

"Oh," I said, winking at her, then taking a drink and looking around the room. "It seems like a popular place."

"It maintains a steady crowd. Been shut down a few times for serving to minors, but somehow they always manage to get their license back."

"Did Jettie like to come here?"

"Never for the nightlife. He and Jeremiah would occasionally come down in the afternoon for a beer or two. But they mostly just enjoyed drinking while they fished, either in a boat on the Arkansas River or at Kerr Lake."

"What about you. Do you like places like this?"

"Not alone. But it's nice to come with someone."

At that moment one of the pool-playing cowboys came up to us with cue stick in hand.

"Howdy, Bella," he said.

He was a toothy looking swain, his face sunburned and freckled and dark red hair seeped from under his hat brim. He reminded me of someone—a celebrity, maybe—but I couldn't come up with the name.

"Hi, Boyd," Bella said.

"How ya been doin'?" he asked.

"Getting along. Boyd, I'd like you to meet Trevor Hodge. He's Jettie's boy."

Boyd's large incisors disappeared behind his lips, but his hesitation was short-lived and he extended his free hand.

"Please to meet you," he said.

"Likewise," I said, shaking his hand. He gripped mine firmly, healthier than I expected. After he let loose of my hand he laughed slightly and looked back at Bella.

"Been thinking about hopping on the bull here in a minute. Be sure and watch."

"I will," she said.

"Maybe we can dance a spell later."

"Maybe."

He touched the front of his hat. "See you around."

We both watched him walk away.

"Friend of yours?" I asked

"Boyd has hit on me for the last ten years. He's harmless."

"What did he mean by hopping on the bull?"

"It's how wannabe cowboys show off." She pointed a finger. "That mechanical bull over there."

She pointed at the contraption that I thought looked like an oversized piece of luggage.

"Mechanical bull?"

"It's the closest you can ever get to the real thing, but like Jettie used to say, it hardly touches the fundamentals."

We each took a drink of beer and I continued to observe the mechanical devise. Suddenly the jukebox quit playing. Bella grabbed my hand and escorted me to the opposite side, near the pool table, where the fancy music-playing machine resided below a poster of a buxom blonde in a bikini and cowboy hat, and in her hand held a longneck bottle of Budweiser.

Bella inserted a dollar bill into the jukebox scanner. "So who do you like to listen to?"

I looked through the glass at the many selections and saw everything from George Strait to Reba McIntire, and oldies like George Jones and Hank Williams. Out of fear of making a bad selection, I decided to let her choose. "Oh, I'm not too picky. You go ahead."

Her first choice was *Cowboy Take Me Away* by the Dixie Chicks, which came over the speaker before she punched in the numbers of her second selection. She made four more selections then we found our way back to the table.

I grabbed the pitcher of beer and refilled our mugs. "So is this a better atmosphere?"

"Perfect."

"Then now you're on the spot. You have to tell me about yourself."

"I wouldn't know where to begin."

"Let's start with where you grew up."

"Talihina."

"I've heard of that town. Isn't that where Jeremiah gets his homemade whiskey?"

"I wouldn't doubt it. I've heard of people having stills up in Winding Stair Mountain."

"Do you still live there?"

"No, I live in Poteau now. I used to work fulltime at the hospital as a nursing assistant. But now I just work part-time in ER, train horses and concentrate on my barrel racing."

"Do you have your own ranch?"

"No, I rent a stable in Poteau. But I've been thinking of buying one, especially now."

"So what was it like growing up in Talihina?"

"My dad worked in a factory over in Wilburton, and he raised quarter horses on the side. That's how I learned to ride."

"Do you still work with your dad?"

"He died when I was still in high school. He was an alcoholic."

"I'm sorry."

"It's okay. You know, it's ironic. My mom was full-blooded Choctaw, and my dad was German/Scottish. Stereotypically, it's usually the Indian that's the drunkard. But my mom hated drinking. I think my father made her hate it."

"That's understandable. And your mom is a hair stylist, right?"

"Yeah, she has a beauty parlor down in Talihina."

"Did she ever remarry?"

"She almost did once, but the guy came home drunk one night. She kicked him out and swore she would never have another man in her life."

"How sad."

"Yeah, well that's my family."

"Were you an only child?"

"Oh, no. I have three older brothers. None of them live around here. My dad drove them all away."

"Sounds like you had a rough childhood."

"Well, let's put it this way. I'd rather die than go through it again."

Suddenly I began to worry about her. It seemed that all her life she had experienced great struggles, a family divided by her father's weak habit, then the habit finally claiming his life, and now, the loss of a man she loved. I was almost afraid to ask her anything more.

"If this is too much for you, we can stop," I said.

"Oh, I've grown kind of rigid over the years. I can handle it."

I wasn't sure I believed her, but then again, she seemed very strong and thus far was doing a great job of opening up to me. And who was to know if she'd ever do it again?

"Besides Jettie," I said, "was there ever anyone else?"

"Yeah, I was married for six months."

I don't know why but this surprised me. Not so much that she had been married, but for such a short period of time.

She continued. "He was a doctor at the hospital where I worked as a nursing assistant. I was young and he was so smooth. He took me out to fancy restaurants. Every now and then we'd fly to Dallas in his plane, spend the whole weekend shopping and dining out. He knew how much I wanted a horse ranch, and he used that to lure me into his life. Making promises he would never keep."

"Why did he do that?"

Her face grew stern and almost pale. "Because all he wanted was a piece of ass. A pretty young Indian trophy wife to hang on his side and make him look good."

"What a jerk."

"Yeah, he was a jerk."

"Well at least it's behind you."

I figured this was enough for now, and tried to change the mood by giving her a smile. "So, you like horses?"

This made her laugh a little. She took a drink of her beer when suddenly the music quit playing and a voice came over a loud speaker and a light shined over the mechanical bull. Then a man in a cowboy hat and a short sleeved western shirt with a belly that hung over his belt walked under the light and spoke into a microphone.

"Ladies and gentlemen, we have a challenge! Boyd Simmons has opted to challenge the bull!"

Several people in the crowd cheered and applauded. The man with the belly walked away and Boyd hopped up on the bull. He had one buckskin glove on his right hand, and he jiggled and squirmed on top the bull as if he were looking for a comfortable position. With the gloved hand he grabbed a single handle that stuck up in front of him. He raised the other hand above his head and nodded to the big-bellied man who stood near him gripping a joystick.

Instantly, the bull started spinning while simultaneously the back end rose up and down. Boyd's free arm swayed with the jerking motions and after several seconds a horn sounded, the bull slowed and the crowd cheered.

As the bull stopped, Boyd jumped off and flashed his big teeth at his admirers. Eventually, his gaze found Bella, and along with his trademark smile he nodded at her.

"Very impressive," I said.

"Hardly," Bella said.

"Why?"

"If he did that on a real bull then he'd earn my respect."

"Why don't he—ride a real bull, that is?"

"Oh he tries. But like I said, a real bull is much different. And besides that, Boyd is a dipshit."

I laughed and instantly realized where she was coming from. A new song started on the jukebox, *Amarillo by Morning* by George Strait. Bella looked into my eyes for a short moment then smiled. "Do you like to dance?"

I looked out into the crowd of people. "Here?"

She gazed out into the crowd as well. "Sure, why not?"

"Whatever you say."

She grabbed my hand and led me to a clear area not far from the jukebox, which was covered with imitation woodgrain tiles. She put her hands around my neck and I held mine around her waist. I gazed back at the seated crowd, but no one seemed to pay any mind to us dancing alone, except Boyd, who gazed at me with a contemptuous half-grin as he walked toward the pool table. So I tried to loosen up and let Bella lead. The song wasn't entirely slow, but it was peaceful enough to catch a comfortable rhythm.

"This was one of Jettie's favorite songs," she said.

I listened to the words and quickly understood that it was about rodeo life. "I guess that makes sense."

"He loved George Strait. Bought every piece of music he ever recorded."

"So Jettie liked music?"

"Sort of. But he didn't care much for the new pop stuff. He liked guys like Keith Whitley, Waylon Jennings, Willie Nelson, and he liked cowboy music from guys like Chris LaDoux Michael Martin Murphy, and Ghost Town Council. Stuff with soul."

"Cool."

"Jettie wasn't a follower. He liked what he liked and that was it."

"That's very admirable."

She leaned back and looked into my eyes. "I'm sure you would have liked him."

"Yeah, well my mom thought differently."

"I didn't know him then, of course, so I can't help you there."

"Yeah, I know. I guess that's why I'm going to have to meet some more people."

"You know I'll help all I can?"

Her eyes seemed soft and compassionate, and like the last time I held her, I was feeling a sense of belonging. I tried to return the same compassion with my own smile, though unsure how successful I would be. "I know you will."

Suddenly the song changed again and now the jukebox played *Ain't Goin' Down (Till The Sun Comes Up)* by Garth Brooks, and other couples began to join us on the dance floor.

She let loose of my waist and grabbed my hands and looked at me with a beguiling stare. "So now do you *really* want to dance?"

"Do I have a choice?"

She grinned and shook her head, then took my hand, raised my arm and twirled around underneath. At first I felt novice and awkward, but decided to let her lead the way, and before long dancing with Bella seemed amazingly simple. So simple that it became second nature, as did the number of beers that kept us going the rest of the night.

FOURTEEN

I knew Jeremiah would be surprised to see me, but from the way he jerked his head and stared, the image of me in a straw cowboy hat and driving Jettie's pickup appeared to disturb him.

He stood outside his machine shop, filling the GMC with gasoline out of a red barrel that lay on its side on top of a tall girded tower. When I stepped out of the truck, Jezebel came from under the GMC and barked at me, but on Jeremiah's command she hushed and went back to her shady post. After he hung the pump nozzle on a wire hook on the tower, he spun the gas cap back on the GMC and gave me the smile I had been waiting for.

"You sure know how to scare the hell out of a man," he said.

"Didn't mean to."

"I thought I was either seeing a ghost or that my whisky hangovers are getting way out of hand."

I chuckled and we shook hands, then I looked back at Jettie's old pickup. "I thought I'd take her for a spin."

"That was Jettie's pride and joy."

"Yeah, and I'm yet to figure out why."

"So, are you here for the weekend?"

"No, for the summer."

He pushed his cowboy hat back and squinted at the light that now covered his face. "No shit? What about your job?"

"There are other jobs."

The expression on his face seemed more relaxed and, in a squinting fashion, his eyes let me know that he was happy with my decision. "Well, you're just in time. I was about to go check for newborns."

"Newborn what?"

"Calves."

He opened the door to the GMC while simultaneously retrieving a cigarette and placing it between his lips. Jezebel darted swiftly from under the truck and leaped almost acrobatically onto the bed, then rested in what seemed to be a favorite spot next to the hay bale. I got in on the passenger side and we drove to one of the far pastures that waved with tall amber grass and where several head of cattle grazed. They were of an assortment of colors—black, red, white, gray, some with white faces, and several with large humps on the backs of their necks and long floppy ears. Many of them had small calves near their sides, which either sucked on their udders or frolicked in the grass.

Jeremiah pointed to a silvery gray cow with a neck hump and floppy ears. "She's about to pop one out," he said.

The black circles around the cow's large glassy eyes gave her a natural and almost profound beauty. Like her eyes, her square black nose offered an attractive contrast to the silvery-white hide that formed over her skull. And her body, though slender and lean in many places, swelled in the center as though she'd swallowed one of Jeremiah's gasoline barrels.

"Interesting looking cow," I said.

"She's a Brahma. I've raised some prize bulls out of that old girl."

As we drew closer the cow turned swiftly; a long string of white snot flew from her nose into the grass and hung there. Then I noticed a thin bloody mass hanging from her backside.

"What's wrong with her?" I asked.

"Her water broke."

"You mean she's about to give birth to a baby cow?"

I wasn't sure why, but Jeremiah chuckled a bit. "Yeah, that's right."

The old cow bawled and strutted away from us, then stopped again and fell slowly to her side. A shiny, wet, bluish, membrane looking lump appeared on her backside. And in a matter of seconds, the wet lump plopped into the grass, unfolded and sprawled its limbs. The old cow went fast back to her feet and turned and licked the newborn.

"Atta girl," Jeremiah said.

"That's one of the coolest things I've ever seen," I said.

"Stick around and you'll see a lot more. About twenty more to go."

"What will you do with all of them?"

"Different things. Some will be used for calf roping, steer wrestling, and when they grow up some will eventually join the cow or bull herd."

"Where will this one end up?"

"When it gets on its feet I'll tell ya."

The mother cow licked the little newborn until thick strands of almost white hair became more visible and it started to look more like a calf than a wet, bloody mass. Eventually it tried to stand, and amazingly, with very few attempts it wobbled to its feet and instinctively to its mother's udder.

"Ah," Jeremiah said. "That could very well be the next Bodacious."

"Say what?"

"Bodacious—the most famous bull that ever bucked inside an arena."

"So that's a bull calf?"

"Yes, sir."

"What's so good about Bodacious?"

"He was a champion, and one of the fiercest bulls in the business. Only seven cowboys ever rode him a full eight seconds. Some wouldn't even ride him."

"That sounds almost counterproductive. What good is he if cowboys won't ride him?"

"To the cowboy, rodeo is a sport and to a few it's a way to make a living. To the rodeo promoters, it's a business. Fans would pile into the arena to see Bodacious. Bottom line, he sold tickets."

"I see. So if you can raise another Bodacious, you can make a lot of money?"

"Well, sorta. I really don't give a damn about the money, I just enjoy the hell out of competing against other stock contractors."

"Sounds like you've almost got your own little side competition going."

"Yeah, I guess I do."

We both watched the newborn suck aggressively; milk frothed around his miniature black mouth. The mother watched attentively as other calves came to inspect their new pasture mate, extending their noses and sniffing at him.

"This is better than the Discovery Channel," I said. "Minus the stalking hyenas, that is."

"No, they're out there."

I gazed to the far reaches of the pasture. "Hyenas?"

"Coyotes."

"Where?"

"Where we can't see them."

"Do they bother the calves?"

"Oh yes."

"That's not good. Is there anything you can do?"

"We do what we can. Me and Jettie and a few of the neighbors used to organize a hunt every so often. We'd kill quite a few but I think they produce ten to every one we kill."

"So I guess ranching has its antagonists?"

"Yes, it does."

Jeremiah continued to drive slowly through the pasture, inspecting the cows and calves along the way. I was suddenly amazed at how content I was riding through the field; attracted to the scenery, the livestock, and the intriguing stories that Jeremiah told. I had never experienced anything so new and different, and ironically the life had always surrounded me without me ever knowing. It made me wonder what life might have been like if I had known my father. If he had taken me on drives through the pasture, teaching me about cattle and bull riding. Even with such a little taste of the life, I already had some understanding of why he would never want to leave it, but the void that still lingered in my mind was why Mom wanted nothing to do with it, and more so, why it eventually killed him.

"What happened in the accident?" I asked.

Jeremiah looked at me, as if frightened by my question. But he took a deep drag off his cigarette then smashed it into the ashtray.

"Jettie got on a bull named Cyclone. It was a young bull and no cowboy had ever succeeded in riding him."

"Was Cyclone like Bodacious? Was he dangerous?"

"No, nothing like Bodacious. No different than any other bull, really."

"So then it was just a freak accident?"

Jeremiah looked at me again, took a deep breath then reached for another cigarette. "There's something you need to know, Trevor. Jettie wasn't killed in an organized event. He was with me on a contracting job down in Fort Worth. He got drunk and accepted some stupid dare."

"He rode a bull drunk?"

"And then some. It was two in the morning. He and a bunch of his old buddies and a few young cowboys got into an argument at a local pub. His old buddies tried to cool him down, but one of the young bucks had him hot and riled. So they all followed him back to the arena and they worked Cyclone into the chute."

"At night?"

"Well, they turned a few of the arena lights on, but it didn't matter. Jettie was drunk, out of focus, and too damned old and out of shape to be riding a bull. That young bull spun so fast out of the chute that Jettie was airborne before the gate had completely opened."

"Did the bull trample him?"

"No, his head hit the gate. From what I understand, it killed him instantly."

"Damn."

Jeremiah exhaled a long stream of smoke through his nose. "Yeah, it wasn't a good night."

"Did you see it happen?"

"No, I was asleep in my camper. Buddy Wells came and woke me and told me they took Jettie to the hospital."

"Did Bella see it?"

"No, thank God. She was in her camper, too. Jodie and I went and got her and we all went to the hospital together. He was already dead."

I tried to absorb all the drama, along with a new taste of Jettie and his behavior. From what I had already learned about him, this almost seemed out of character. But then again, I could remember a few instances when alcohol challenged every bit of my good sense.

"I'm sorry if this was difficult for you to talk about," I said.

"No, you needed to know."

"Suddenly there's a lot I feel like I need to know. And I still don't quite know how to handle the inheritance."

"Well, there's no hard feelings in this family."

"And that amazes me."

"Oh, why?"

"Well, I heard you and Jettie were close. Why didn't he give you the money?"

Jeremiah smirked a bit. "You're right, we were close, which is why he knew I didn't need the money. Plus, I understood why he did it. In a way, it made him feel like a real father."

"It's the nicest thing anyone has ever done for me."

"Then just accept it as that. And if you're not sure what to do with the money, then don't do anything. It'll do nothing but grow where it's at."

"I also don't know what to tell you about my interest in this ranch. I kind of like it. It's sure a lot nicer to look at than a bank statement."

"You definitely have Hodge blood."

"Why is that?"

"The land and the life have always been more important. But some folks have a rough go at making money on their ranches and end up losing them to foreclosure. The business is very volatile anymore." He looked at me and grinned. "Which is why I'm glad I bought a little of that Wal-Mart stock, too."

"Cool. Did you fare as well as Jettie?"

He continued to smile. "Let's put it this way. For every dollar of stock Jettie bought, I bought five."

All I could do was smile and Jeremiah eventually laughed out loud. It was apparent that this lost family of mine were either naturals at managing money, or just damned lucky. And from the modest way they lived, they didn't flaunt it in a way that would come across as offensive to others. All Jeremiah seemed to care about was his family, his livestock, and the peaceful scenery around him. Never before had I known such a man, and in an uncanny way, his humble nature made me feel right at home.

FIFTEEN

I spent the entire Sunday with Jeremiah on the ranch, observing how he inspected the livestock, logged the newborns into a ledger, and even documented those that needed special medical attention. I was impressed at how much he knew; especially that he performed his own veterinarian work. Later in the afternoon we saddled two horses out of several in a fenced pasture near the house. Jeremiah's was tall and tan colored with a black mane and tail. He said it was a buckskin, and a gelding, and that its name was Francisco.

He pointed out several others that had belonged to Jettie, particularly three of his favorite geldings. He said that Jettie knew horses pretty well, and that they all served certain purposes. There was a sorrel he'd called Dancer because of the graceful manner in which it moved its feet, and which he used for cutting cattle. And there was a stout dapple-gray named Floyd that he used for fun riding, and his name came about when Jettie first saw it as a colt, and commented that it was such a "pretty boy". Then there was a red roan named Jack, who from his versatility was deemed a "Jack of all trades" and was a backup for both horses. I also learned that the names were just everyday handles for the horses, that their registered names were much different, but too awkward to use on an everyday basis.

Since we were going to sort and bring in a few cows and calves that needed medical attention, Jeremiah helped me saddle Dancer. He demonstrated to me how and where to lay the thick saddle blanket, position the saddle, and how to attach and tighten the cinch. It wasn't a lot to remember, but I could tell that getting it right would take some practice.

I was amazed at how well I rode, even though it felt awkward at the start. But the point of view from horseback gave me a feeling of sovereignty, as if I now had some superlative control over everything around me. Then again, as I looked at the tall grasses waving in the breeze like a rippling blanket, at the colorful birds in the air and in the trees, and at the livestock and swarms of flies and gnats that swirled around them, I realized that I was very much like them—a mere electron in the great atom of life.

The sorrel that carried me was a beautiful animal, with a blonde mane and tail and a sure-footed gentleness about him. I developed an instant fondness for him and wondered if all horses gave their riders such a rare sense of security.

Jezebel came along and I was able to experience her at work for the first time. I had never seen an animal so intense and serious. Somehow, she knew exactly which animal Jeremiah wanted to cut out of the herd. She ran swiftly to whichever side of the animal was necessary, and by barking at its feet forced it to head the proper direction.

Not having a clue what to do, I did only what Jeremiah instructed me to do, which for the most part was stay back and out of the way. But when the work was done Jeremiah and I rode on each side of our small sorted herd while Jezebel made sure none ran astray. For the most part, the cattle seemed to know where to go, and eventually we ended up in a rectangular corral near the machine shop.

At one corner of the corral was a red metal contraption, what Jeremiah called a squeeze chute. My job was to send a cow or calf, one at a time into the device, and when it was far enough in, Jeremiah pulled a large lever that closed around the animal's neck and restrained them. Some of the cattle fought the contraption like hell, kicking and bawling, while others seemed to be very good patients.

A couple of the cows each had one bad eye that, unlike the good one, was clouded over by a pink or purplish film. Jeremiah said it was pinkeye, naturally, and that the cows needed to be injected with an antibiotic. I thought I would fall off my horse in a dizzy awe when I watched him grab a large syringe and stick the needle under the cows eyelid. But from her bawling reaction, I'm sure the old girl was much more uncomfortable with the method than I was. In fact, by the way she raised her tail and emptied her bowels, I believed in her own way she told Jeremiah exactly how she felt about his doctoral methods.

And when the little calves went into the chute, Jeremiah tagged their ears with a plastic yellow tag printed with large black numbers, and also, using a needled device, he tagged the back of the same ear with what he called a hormone implant. He said it was kind of like Miracle Grow for cattle.

When we were all done the cattle remained in a small fenced area on the other side of the corral, an area Jeremiah called the "sick pen". This is where the cattle remained so he could keep a close watch on their eyes to make sure they healed properly, then once healed he would release them back into the herd.

We took the horses back to the horse barn, removed the saddles and bridles and returned them to the tack area, then released the horses back to the pasture.

Jeremiah opened a small cabinet in the tack area and removed a pint bottle of his homemade potion, removed the cap and took a drink. As he puckered his lips and held the liquid inside his mouth, he handed the bottle to me. Though the idea of taking another drink of that awful stuff scared the hell out of me, I at least knew what I was up against and that sipping would be less likely to cause any physical trauma. So I accepted the bottle and took a small sip. Though still very bitter this round was much easier to handle.

I handed the bottle back to him and he retired to a square bale of hay. He leaned back against the barn wall, removed his hat and set it beside him on the hay bale. His hair was sweaty and indented where the hat had been, and his face looked hot and tired. He pulled the pack of cigarettes from his shirt pocket and lit one.

"It's been an interesting afternoon," I said. "Thank you for including me."

"Your welcome," he said. "But there's really no including you in something that's part yours in the first place."

"Yeah, well, I guess that part hasn't totally soaked in yet."

We sat in silence for a moment. I sensed that something bothered Jeremiah, but then again we had been working so I figured he was just tired.

"I spent yesterday with Bella," I said.

He nodded as smoke streamed from his nostrils. "Fine gal, that Bella."

"Yeah, I like her."

"She didn't try to sell you on that Wrangler jean bullshit, did she?"

I grunted slightly. "Yeah, she tried."

"Besides being a little misguided about things, Bella would have made Jettie a fine wife."

"You really think she's misguided?"

"Oh, I don't know. It may just be that she's from a younger generation. Nothing bothers me more than to hear some greenhorn flap their jaws like they know more than people with experience do. They need to open their ears and shut their mouths."

"I don't recall Bella being that way."

"She's not as bad as most. But so many times she'd come around, crying to me and Jodie because Jettie won't commit. 'What can I do! What can I do!' she'd say. We tried to tell her that she was digging for gold in a mine that had already seen too much dynamite. But she wouldn't listen, and I got tired of hearing her weep."

"She's had a pretty rough life. Maybe her search for peace is wearing her out."

"Yeah, you're probably right. And like all of us, it hurt like hell to see Jettie crumble."

"Crumble?"

He glanced at me with his tired eyes, as if he regretted getting started. He took another drink from the pint and looked out into the daylight. "I've seen a lot of bull riders in my life, but I never seen one better than my own brother. And I ain't biased, neither.

"I remember the first time he made it to the National Finals. I swear that Jodie and I were more excited than he was. He did well until he got to the last ride. He drew a bull that was very predictable, and that bull came out of the chute exactly like he knew it would."

"What happened?"

"He fell off in the first spin—as if there was grease in his goddamn saddle."

"Do you know why?"

His face reddened and he glared back at me. "Hell no! And that wasn't the first time. He'd go to NFR five more times, only to repeat that same embarrassing ride as if it were some canned performance!"

"Did you ever talk to him about it?"

"He'd just as soon have a knife fight than talk about it. And before he ever had a chance to figure it out, he got too old and out of shape to compete."

"Bella said that he worked out and stayed in shape."

This made him laugh a bit. "Trevor, when you reach forty, you can lift and run all you want, but none of that is going to fool Mother Nature."

"I see. Well, hopefully the answer is out there some-where."

He looked sternly at me. "What good would that do now?"

"Are you saying you wouldn't like to know?"

We stared in silence for a moment, then he looked back toward the pasture. "Hell, I don't know. There's times I'd just as soon forget all of it."

"Well, Jeremiah, I can keep it all to myself if you want, but I came down here to learn who my father was. And I can't leave until I know."

He looked back at me and I held my candor. And from the way he relaxed his expression, I was sure he understood, or at least respected my commitment.

He stood and patted me on the shoulder and didn't say another word about it. He invited me in for supper and for the rest of the evening I enjoyed a fine meal and a quiet time with him and Jodie. She too was pleased to know I decided to stay the summer, and insisted that I ride along to all the rodeos where they were providing livestock. The idea fit in very well with my reason for being here, so I accepted.

I returned to Jettie's house after dark, took a hot shower and changed into a pair of cotton boxer shorts and a clean T-shirt. My body was tired from riding, especially my crotch, groin, and lower back. The hot shower had felt very soothing to my aching muscles and joints, and since Bella was coming over in the morning to start our workout routine, I figured it was best to get some rest.

When my head hit the pillow, I stared at the white textured ceiling now shadowed by the sheer drapes that filtered the streetlight, and my mind wandered into a recap of the weekend. I saw myself riding Dancer in the pasture, Bella rounding the barrels in the arena, and her and I dancing at The Oasis. I closed my eyes and smiled and couldn't remember a bed feeling so good.

SIXTEEN

I spent most of the week helping Jeremiah prepare for the Hugo Rodeo in Hugo, Oklahoma, and occasionally a little time with Bella at the Spiro arena while she ran time trials.

Our daily, alternating workout routine proved to be helpful in both settings since my physical endurance was put to a test each day. If it wasn't unloading, positioning or reloading steel barrels into the back of a pickup truck, it was sorting calves and bulls on the ranch. I don't think my body had ever been in such great shape, nor had it ever been so fatigued at the end of a workday.

The Hugo Rodeo was an important event for Jeremiah and Bella. Jeremiah contracted to provide both bulls and roping calves and Bella needed badly to acquire more points for the futurity.

Thursday afternoon and evening Jodie packed the camper with enough living necessities for three days, while Jeremiah, Bella and I loaded the storage compartments on the stock trailers with hay, feed, tack and medical supplies. Wednesday we had worked the stock into their own special pens for easy loading, and come Friday morning that was the last of our tasks before heading down the road to Hugo.

Besides the gooseneck camper that was to be our home for the weekend, six other trailers were utilized to haul the stock. Jeremiah owned two of them, regular stock trailers that he pulled with pickups, and the others were owned by local ranchers or trucking companies hired for transport. Two were trailers like Jeremiah's, and the others, long and two-tiered, pulled by semi trucks. One of Jeremiah's trailers, which he said was his pride and joy, was a thirty-three-foot-long Sundowner, and unlike any piece of equipment I had ever seen before. It was white with red and silver graphic striping and tinted windows near the top. On one side, a large door opened from the top and hinged at the bottom, making a ramp for horses to go inside. And inside were stalls for five horses, with feedbags and rubber looking mats on the floors and walls. Near the front of the trailer was a single door for human beings and a small area equipped like a penthouse suite, which included a mini refrigerator filled mostly with alcoholic beverages. After touring that section, I quickly realized why it was Jeremiah's pride and joy.

The Sundowner carried all of our personal horses. Bella's horse, a bay she called Freedom Run, was tied in the back next to Francisco. I decided to take Floyd since I'd be riding mostly for fun. And Jodie took her own horse, Chantilly, a Palomino mare that she said reminded her of a porcelain figurine she once had from Chantilly, France.

Once all the stock was loaded, the caravan of trucks and trailers headed south toward Poteau. From Jeremiah and Bella's efficient methods of organization and concentration, I could almost feel the excitement and adrenaline circulate through the air. Jeremiah pulled the Sundowner with a Ford diesel-powered truck with dual tires. The truck matched the trailer in color and striping and created a remarkable presence on the highway. I rode with Bella as she drove the white GMC that pulled the stock trailer of bulls and calves, and Jodie drove another Ford pickup that pulled the Coach-men camper.

We drove through the Talihina Mountains and Bella pointed out the little town where she was raised. The mountains reminded me of the Boston Mountains in Arkansas, only a smaller range with mostly pine trees rather than oaks.

Other than the short stop Jeremiah made to replenish his homemade liquor supply, we drove straight through to Hugo and arrived at the arena before sunset. We unloaded all the stock and moved them to their assigned pens and parked the camper and other trailers in their designated spots behind the arena. Tired from our busy day, Jeremiah and Jodie decided to retire early, but Bella and I still had enough energy to find one of Hugo's local honkytonks.

A cowboy at the arena directed us to a joint called The Crossing, which sat near the north bank of the Red River. The Red River marked the boundaries of southern Oklahoma and northeast Texas, which caused The Crossing to pull a mixed crowd of residents from both states. The cowboy at the arena warned us that because of the mixed crowd, The Crossing got pretty rowdy at times, but Bella and I saw no reason for trouble to come our way.

The Crossing was three times the size of The Oasis, with a large square dance floor in the center, two large bars on each end, six pool tables, several waitresses in short denim skirts, cowboy hats and white boots, and a DJ that played the latest in country music. But like The Oasis, it had a single mechanical bull near the dance floor that was already spinning and throwing wannabe cowboys onto the cushioned mats below.

The waitress brought us a pitcher of beer and I picked up the tab while Bella poured. A clamor of hollers erupted near the mechanical bull and I immediately recognized Boyd jiggling and positioning himself on the seat.

"You know, I just figured out who he reminds me of."

"Boyd?"

"He looks like a skinny John Elway."

"Trevor, that is a huge insult to John Elway."

"It would be if we were comparing personalities, but I'm talking about looks."

"Still, Boyd is no charm."

Reminiscent of The Oasis, Boyd rode the simulated device for the full eight seconds without even a hint that he was struggling to hold on. The crowd of cowboys cheered and high-fived him as he stepped off.

"He's such a showboat," Bella said. "And stupid, too. If he got hurt, that could ruin his chances at Hugo."

"He's riding in Hugo?"

"He always does."

"Maybe he's just practicing?"

"Well, I wish him luck."

In the midst of all his buddies, he looked our way as if he almost knew, telepathically, that we were talking about him.

"Don't look now," I said, "but I think he's coming over here."

"Great," Bella said sarcastically.

He came to our table with the grandiloquence of a gamecock. And as he smiled at us, I knew I was right about the John Elway resemblance.

"Howdy, Bella," he said, placing his hands on his hips.

"Hi, Boyd."

"Did you see me ride?"

"Yes, congratulations."

He looked at me as though my very presence, even in silence, was interfering with whatever plan he had in his head.

"Does Jettie's boy ride?"

"Ride what?" I quickly asked.

He grunted and raised one corner of his mouth, then looked again at Bella. "Now, Bella, haven't you shown this city boy what a bull is yet?"

Before Bella could respond, and assuming where he was trying to go with his question, I quickly answered for her. "I just wanted to be sure you were talking about a *real* bull or that gyrating piece of luggage out there."

His half smile drooped and his eyes lit up as though powered by some kind of flammable liquid.

"I take it you don't think much of our mechanical friend out there?"

"I never said that. I was just giving you back a piece of your own insult."

He revealed all of his teeth this time, and a laugh to go along with them. The cowboy hat and the atmosphere didn't make his persona any different than that of other egomaniacs I had known. It didn't matter whether it was sports, drama, accounting, or any other profession, someone somewhere competed for something and they each had similar ways of going about. In Boyd's case he had little confidence in his own talents and tried to rely more on competing psychologically as an edge over his opponent. And in this case it wasn't about who was better on the bull, real or mechanical, it was about impressing Bella. The bull was only a tool and he was sure he had me there, but I supposed I knew Bella better than he did and decided to have a little fun.

"You got yourself a real smart mouth, city boy," Boyd said.

"At least I use my brain before operating it."

"Guy's," Bella said, "there's no need for this."

"Maybe we should just step outside and talk about this," he said.

"Step outside?" I said, "And I suppose that means you would want to fight—maybe?"

"No, it'd be more like me givin' you an ass kickin'."

Though I knew it was wrong, I couldn't help but feel the desire to take this cowboy up on his game. Especially since my body felt firm and in shape, and the adrenaline that had enhanced the viscosity of my blood gave me an urge to do something physical. But the last time I hit another human being, and saw the blood rush from the kid's nose, I swore I'd never do it again. I was only ten, and the kid was antagonizing me just as Boyd was doing now. Though in many ways he had gotten what he deserved, I felt an immediate sense of remorse and sorrow for the kid, and it has stuck with me since that day. So I had made a personal pact to deal with disputes in a different manner, and even in Boyd's regard, I knew there had to be a better way to settle whatever differences we had.

"Well, I couldn't stand the humiliation of you kicking my ass, so why don't we try something a little more civil?"

"Guys," Bella said, "stop it!"

"Alright," he said. He removed one hand from his hip and pointed a thumb over his shoulder. "How about the bull?"

Just as I looked at the bull, a short, chubby cowboy flew backwards, his straw cowboy hat adrift, and he fell headfirst into the mat.

"Trevor, don't," Bella said.

Though the object and its nature were completely foreign to me, it did offer the physical qualities that could at least appease my hormonal yearning. But Boyd had a tremendous edge. I would have to stay on for eight seconds and at the same level of gyration that Boyd had mastered. The odds were that I'd most likely lose, but for some strange reason I really didn't care. My loss would only be in competition with Boyd, and not likely that Bella would care regardless the outcome.

"Okay, let's do it."

Boyd offered the biggest smile yet.

Bella fumed. "Trevor! What the hell are you doing?"

"Be at the bull in five minutes," Boyd said, then walked away.

"You're an idiot," she said.

"What are you talking about?"

"He'll kick your ass on that thing."

"Who cares?"

I almost sensed a hint of disappointment in her stare. "And you could get hurt."

"Oh, thank you. Like Boyd, now you've insulted me."

"Insulted you?"

"Yeah, little city boy don't know what he's doing."

"Those things are dangerous, Trevor."

"Bella, this is a bar. That is a device to entertain. And you even said that it is nothing like the real thing."

"Trevor, before you get on that thing you have to go up to the operator and sign a disclaimer, which in a roundabout way says that they won't be held responsible if you break your fucking neck!"

As I watched another cowboy get thrown, hold his shoulder and grimace as he stood up, I knew there was a lot of substance to what Bella was saying. But Boyd and his buddies looked up at me, grinning and laughing at what I'm sure was their predetermined outcome. Whether Bella was right or not, I had already put myself on the spot, and no matter where you're from, it's better to lose than to be a coward.

SEVENTEEN

I didn't need to read the disclaimer; I already knew the basis as to what it said, which, quite frankly meant that they made money off this dangerous mechanism, and if you wanted to risk paralysis or death then that was your business. So I signed the document and paid the operator ten bucks for the privilege of risking my life, or death, whichever way I chose to look at it.

Bella still thought I was an idiot, but there was obviously a bit of stubborn redneck in my blood because I wasn't about to back down from this boy now no matter what she said. And I bargained with Boyd a little, asking for a practice ride since he definitely had a huge edge when it came to experience. By the way he gloated I sensed this fed his ego, and he agreed to my request without much hesitation. But I still lacked the knowledge of technique and no one seemed eager to come forward and offer any advice. All Bella knew was what she had overheard Jettie say, but his past comments always pertained to real bulls and a particular move that animal was famous for doing. Depending on the operator, the mechanical bull could do about anything, so the only advice Bella could offer was to sit straight, don't lean backward, use my raised arm for balance, and keep my butt in the center of gravity. At this point, "gravity" was a word I really didn't care to hear.

I borrowed a buckskin glove for my left hand from a cardboard box near the operator's booth, then positioned myself on the bull. For a moment I began to believe that Bella was right because I felt like an absolute idiot. Straddling this thing was more than just awkward or uncomfortable, I was the proverbial fish out of water. Nevertheless, I took a deep breath, looked at Bella, and suddenly noticed that every single eyeball in the joint looked my way. The damn music even stopped playing. But I couldn't stop now, and I had to realize that this was my practice ride, so I took a second breath then nodded to the operator.

The back of the bull raised and I felt as if I was going to slide all the way forward and on to the mat, but then it jerked hard and spun left and the next I knew I was face-first on the vinyl mat below. All I heard was laughter, and when I looked up, the entire crowd looked at me as if I was some sort of pathetic imbecile. For a short moment I wondered if they weren't right. But Bella didn't laugh; she just covered her eyes and eventually peeked out at me and shook her head. I quickly decided that it didn't matter what people thought, that this was just a game, and that I had to crawl back up on the device and give it my best shot.

I found my hat, put it back on, and crawled back up on the bull. To my left Boyd stood smiling, his arms crossed, and no doubt anxiously waiting for me to humiliate myself again.

"You can quit now if you want," he said.

"Not a chance," I said.

Bella came up to me. "Trevor, you don't have to do this."

"I'm doing it!"

She stepped back slowly and I tried to recollect what I could have done different. It happened so fast that I couldn't remember a thing about posture or balance, just the fact that the thing felt like a Tilt-A-Whirl at the midway carnival, that went up and down besides going around. The up and down part didn't seem so bad, it was when it spun that caught me off guard. So I kept in my mind the image of a Tilt-A-Whirl, thinking that if I just concentrated on the spinning, that I could handle the bucking part.

I raised my arm again and this time decided not to look into the crowd. *Tilt-A-Whirl. Tilt-A-Whirl.* I kept repeating it in my mind.

I nodded to the operator and this time the bull bucked and spun at the same time. Amazingly, I stayed on, but then again, I was not on a mechanical bull, I was in a Tilt-A-Whirl car and the crowd around me was nothing more than a mass of laughing and screaming carnival patrons. I kept spinning and jerking back and forth, my stomach feeling the fuzzy impacts. I became a part of the device, as if my buttocks were somehow fastened to the seat, but still very maneuverable. Then came a buzzer, and the feel of the car slowing. The applauding crowd slowly brought me back to the real scene.

When the bull stopped I stared dizzily at the crowd around me who still cheered and applauded noisily. I focused my eyes on Bella as she shook her head and eventually smiled. Then I found Boyd, who sneered like he'd just lost at a high-stakes poker game, then shouted out above the crowd.

"Do it again! At the highest level!"

The operator, an older man in a black felt hat and western shirt with an image of fire flames printed on the shoulders, shook his head at Boyd. "That was the highest level."

"Bullshit!" Boyd yelled, then ran to the booth. He looked down at the control panel then raised his head and glared at me again. Then he pointed his finger at me. "This ain't over, jackass!"

"Why not? You made the terms."

After a long stare he stomped away, shoving chairs and other cowboys before finding his own chair and guzzling down a beer. Several of his friends joined him and tried to cool him down, but he cursed at them and continued to glare at me.

"I don't believe what I just saw," Bella said as I hopped down from the bull. "How'd you do it?"

"Hell if I know."

She grabbed my hand and led me away toward our table. Though the challenge may have not been necessary, there was a cool satisfaction having triumphed over Boyd, but from the way Bella smiled and held my hand, the reward of getting the girl was that much better.

We enjoyed our beers while I tried to explain to Bella about the Tilt-A-Whirl. I'm not sure she really understood, in fact, she was more likely to believe that I was some sort of a natural—a genetic quality passed down from my father.

"I wonder how I'd handle a real bull?"

"You're not seriously considering it, are you?"

"Maybe."

"Trevor, don't let that ride make your head swell. I told you that a real bull is much different, and if you don't believe me, just ask Jeremiah."

"Forget it. It was just an idea."

Though I may have eased her mind, I certainly wasn't going to forget it. Like the desire to come here and experience the life, I now felt as if I needed to advance to a new level of learning. If I was going to see matters from Jettie's point of view, then actually feeling the challenge and fear of bull riding may be necessary. But suddenly I realized that it was more than that. Something about the point of competition and feel of the ride stimulated me. Similar to how the town of Spiro once lured me, I was now facing a different fascination, and this one had horns.

EIGHTEEN

T he grand entry was exactly that. I had never seen so many horses and cowboy hats in one place at one time. Nearly everyone who participated in the rodeo, and then some, rode their horse in what seemed an infinitive single file line that began in the livestock area, ran through the main entrance of the arena, along the inside of the fence completely around the oval, and back into the livestock area. All the riders waved and smiled at the crowd like prom queens on parade floats, while music suitable for marching played over the loud speaker and the rodeo announcer introduced certain VIP's.

Jeremiah rode in the lead, Jodie behind him, then me riding Floyd, and Bella behind me. Except Bella, who had her own attire, we all wore red denim shirts with "Hodge Farms" embroidered in white letters on the back. And as we entered the arena, the announcer called out: "Jeremiah Hodge and wife Jodie of Hodge Farms, part of the stock contracting team for the Hugo Rodeo." Then, the big surprise, "Trevor Hodge, the son of the legendary bull rider, Jettie Hodge." I'm sure my face turned a nice pink blush when the crowd applauded. How the hell did the announcer know? Jodie turned around and winked at me, and suddenly I knew.

Bella came up beside me and whispered. "Smile and wave. Those applause are for you."

Though I felt very silly, I did as she instructed. But I wasn't sure I agreed with her. These people didn't even know me, they knew Jettie, and they applauded for him. As I looked across the crowd, I noticed people smile and wave back at me. One man gave me thumbs up then clapped over his head. Two young boys held up their autographed photo of Jettie and waved at me. And one attractive young woman held up a white poster with colorful letters that read, "We miss you Jettie." And around the arena there was more of the same.

We had marched almost half the circumference of the arena when something didn't feel right. I started to squirm and realized my saddle was loose, and the next I knew the saddle started to slide and I found myself on the arena floor, my elbows and butt pressed into the soft red dirt. Laughter erupted from the crowd, and the announcer took advantage of the incident as well.

"Well folks," he said, "we forgot to introduce Trevor Hodge as our official dirt tester for tonight's rodeo."

The crowd seemed very amused by his quick wit, but I saw no humor in it at all.

Jeremiah and Jodie had stopped and looked back at me. Bella dismounted to help.

"Are you okay," she said, laughing at me.

"I don't see anything funny."

We pulled the horse aside while the parade continued around us. Jodie stayed on her horse while Jeremiah dismounted to help put the saddle back on.

"I wonder how that happened," I said. "I'm sure I had the cinch on right."

"You did," Jeremiah said. "I inspected it after you saddled him."

I glanced toward the end of the arena where grand entry riders were entering and exiting, and saw Boyd and several other cowboys riding in, pointing and laughing at me.

"I think I know," I said, thinking back to before the grand entry. After I had saddled Floyd, the way Jeremiah had taught me, I left him tied to the back of the trailer while Jeremiah and I went to the concession stand to get something to eat. When we came back, I noticed Boyd and two of his buddies walking away, snickering, but the idea of them tampering with my saddle never occurred to me—until now.

Jeremiah and Bella followed my gaze.

"What a childish prank," Bella said.

"You think Boyd did this?" Jeremiah asked.

"Don't worry about it," I said. "We're even now."

After we made sure the saddle was secure, we remounted and worked our way back into the march. The crowd applauded and the announcer asked me if the dirt tested positive. I played along and raised my thumb.

"Ladies and gentlemen," he said, "let's have a round of applause for our official dirt tester!"

The crowd went along with the joke and I couldn't wait to get the hell out of the arena.

After we put our horses away, Jeremiah and Jodie went to their special VIP seating. I stayed with Bella to help her prepare for her event. She wrapped a royal blue fabric above the horse's feet that she said gave its legs more support.

"You're not really gonna stand for that, are you?" she asked.

"I humiliated him a little last night, so I suppose we're even now."

"You won fair and square. He had no right to do that."

"But if I retaliate then he'll think he's getting to me and the game goes on and on. Ignoring him will probably piss him off more than if I got him back."

"You obviously don't know cowboys very well."

"How's that?"

"If you don't respond, then you're a wimp."

"Then I guess I'm a wimp."

She looked at me as though I had confessed to some closet shortcoming.

"Remember who just saw you fall," she said. "Everyone in Hugo! And before long the whole town will know that Boyd got the best of you."

"You can't be serious. That's childish!"

"Maybe so, but it's also reality."

I quickly realized that she *was* serious, and that I probably should take her word for whatever consequences I might be facing.

"All right, so what should I do?"

"I'm not saying I have the answer, I'm just saying that you have to do something or you'll never live it down."

The thought of concentrating on such foolishness made me angry. And it made me think about how a similar group of cowboys dared Jettie, which turned out to be fatal in his case. This was more than just a sport or profession, it was a way of life, and the effects of it all occurred inside and outside the arena.

I escorted Bella to the gate area, then joined Jeremiah and Jodie in the VIP seats. We sat just to the right and above the chute area, and luckily for me, in plain view of Boyd and all the other cowboys as they prepared for their event.

Though I could hear their heckles, I did my best to ignore them and watched the barrel racers as they performed.

Jeremiah leaned to me. "You mind telling me what's going on?"

"Nothing I can't handle."

"That might be foolish of you."

I figured I might as well appease him. "Boyd has this thing for Bella, and I guess I'm in his way."

"I see. Well just remember that you've entered another world down here, and cowboys like Boyd like to protect their turf. Especially when they feel intimidated."

"Yeah, and it's my fault."

"Why is that?"

"At first he wanted to fight, but I talked him into a different method to settle our differences."

"What method was that?"

After I told Jeremiah the complete story, all he could do was laugh and finally agree that I had myself in a genuine cowboy predicament.

"How do I get myself out of a 'genuine cowboy predicament'?"

"There's only one way, and that's play along until you're both tired and call a truce."

"I guess Jettie never had the chance to call a truce."

This comment seemed to catch Jeremiah off guard. "How does this have anything to do with what happened to your pa?"

"It all started with a dare. If Jettie would have just walked away he'd be alive today."

"Yeah, you're right. But there's a big difference between having a little fun and going so far as to risking your life. Those young bucks that dared your pa were dumb and foolish. They knew how to get Jettie riled and they get their amusement out of seeing people get hurt."

"Somehow I think Boyd is the same way. He's not going to stop until he sees me bleeding and cowering like a child."

"Then that's where you need to stay sober and keep your head on straight."

"Well, then I guess I have nothing to worry about."

Jeremiah chuckled and patted my shoulder. I'm sure he believed me, but I'm not so sure I believed myself. Not only did I have the pressure from Bella to settle matters with Boyd, but I had this new desire to be more like Jettie, even if it meant taking over his dares.

NINETEEN

Bella did fabulous in her barrel racing event, scoring a 16.12 and the best ride of the evening. We all met her in the livestock area to congratulate her. I had found a vendor selling roses and bought her two; a yellow one for the win and for the friendship that she had shown me since my arrival, and a red one for the love she had shown my father. I didn't bother explaining the color association to her, I figured that their common symbolic meaning was already enough. Regardless, I could see in her eyes and from her smile that she appreciated the gesture.

The next event was the saddle bronc competition and Jeremiah explained to me the history of how it all began on the ranges of the Old West, and how it evolved to such a renowned contest. The image of the bucking horse and the cowboy that rode it brought back memories of the painting by Frederic Remington in Jeremiah and Jodie's living room. I was impressed by the painting then, but even more so now as I observed the portrayal in action.

After the saddle bronc competition, the calf roping event took over the arena. Having spent so much time sorting them on the ranch, I recognized every one of the little critters that came charging out of their special tunnel. I even felt a little sorry for the harmless creatures as the cowboy charged after them on his horse, threw a rope around their neck, then jumped off and tied their legs together with a rope that he'd held in his teeth. Jeremiah said the rope in the cowboy's teeth was a "piggin' strang", which had me a bit perplexed, not just from his dialect, but wondering where the pig came into the picture. But I just let it go.

Regardless of the treatment of the calf, the method and talent of both roper and horse were very impressive. The coordination that had to be required to ride and throw a rope, then jump off, keep one's balance and manhandle the animal to tie its legs together, would place anyone who had never seen it before in a state of awe. But if those weren't enough reasons to be impressed, to observe how the horse stepped backward and kept the rope tight for the cowboy as he tied the calf, really had me shaking my head. This event alone gave me an added appreciation for the people and animals of this sport.

After the conclusion of the calf roping event, hard rock music began to play over the loud speaker, and the announcer added a bit of excitement to his voice which made all the fans stand up and cheer.

It was time for the bulls.

Jeremiah wanted me to get a little more from this next event than just a good view from the VIP seats so he took me down to the chute area where all the cowboys prepared to ride. Boyd appeared to be a little surprised to see me, but even more so when Jeremiah asked him for a minute of his time.

"What's up, Jeremiah?" Boyd asked with a slight quiver in his voice.

"Let's cut through the shit, Boyd."

I already disliked the situation. I felt as if Jeremiah was trying to deal with my problem, like an overprotective daddy, and even a city boy like me knew that such a stand could turn out to be a political nightmare.

Jeremiah continued. "Now I don't know what you and Trevor got against each other, and quite frankly I don't give a rat's ass. But if you ever fuck with any of my livestock or tack again I'll make sure you never ride another bull in a PRCA organized event. You understand, cowboy?"

"Yessir."

"And don't forget, them's my bulls you're ridin', so the game you started is one you'd never win."

This made Boyd swallow, and then he nodded.

"All right," Jeremiah said. "Now if you and Trevor want to beat the shit out of each other, then go do it. Just keep it out of the goddamn arena."

Though it seemed that Jeremiah didn't try to fight my war, I don't imagine he really was too concerned about his tack or livestock. Nevertheless, the differences between Boyd and I were still very much in the open and yet to be resolved.

Boyd gave me a hard stare then went back to his fellow cowboys. Jeremiah and I climbed up on a gate and watched the bulls come down their narrow isle and into their designated chute.

"You wouldn't really do anything to Boyd's bull, would you?"

Jeremiah grinned. "No, but he don't know that."

The beastly animal that came in the chute below us snorted and pounded his stubby horns and sinewy flesh against the fence rails and I could feel the vibration all the way to my bones. Jeremiah said that he was an F1/Brindle, which F1 described the breed, the first result of mixing two purebreds, and brindle the tan and grayish, almost tiger-like streaks of its hide. He also said the bull's name was Rock Solid.

A stocky young cowboy rested his feet on a rail on each side of Rock Solid. Black leather chaps with fancy red and white lettering and red fringe hanging from the edges covered his short legs. He wore a straw cowboy hat with sweat stains above the hatband, several dirt stains on the brim, and a small rectangular Bud Light logo stuck on the side of the crown. The evening air was muggy and sweat beads had formed on the cowboy's forehead and were now starting to run down his face. Over his plaid western shirt he wore a thick black vest, that looked similar to a bulletproof vest I'd seen cops wear in the movies, which also had Bud Light logos on the front and a paper sign pinned on the back that indicated the cowboy's contestant number.

Once the bull seemed to settle, the cowboy lowered himself onto the animal's back. The bull let everyone around him know that he disapproved of the cowboy's position by jerking his powerful body against the fences and trying to buck. I watched the cowboy closely—the intensity in his facial expression was enough to realize just how serious an attempt like this was, and also how much courage was required to follow through. It also made me think of Jettie and his fatal ride, and how a drunk person had no business on an animal like the beast below me now.

The cowboy gripped his left-gloved hand under a handle on a rope somehow attached behind and around the bull's thick, bulbous neck. With his free hand, he beat on the rope to make sure the tightness was to his liking, then raised the hand above his head.

"Remember, Freddy," another cowboy said to the rider. "This bull just likes to buck."

Freddy nodded. "All right, let's do it."

Tom Sawyer by Rush played over the loud speaker, the gate flew open, and the bull had almost turned a full circle into the arena before the gate swung completely open. Clowns tried to tempt the bull but it seemed to ignore their presence. Like the coaching cowboy had said, Rock Solid bucked with very little spin action and Freddy handled the ride like a champ.

When the whistle sounded, Freddy jumped off and landed on his feet and raised his hands in the air. The bull snorted and flung a long string of saliva at one of the clowns but eventually saw the open gate and took his temperament back into the stock area.

The announcer asked the crowd for a round of applause for a great ride from Freddy Jiles of Waco, Texas. But when the official score came across the scoreboard the crowd booed, and

Freddy kicked dirt with his boot and walked out of the arena an angry cowboy.

"Is 88 a bad score?" I asked.

"No," Jeremiah said, "but it's not good enough to win."

"I don't understand. If he rode the full eight seconds, then why didn't he score better?"

"A lot depends on the judges and what the bull does, but I can tell you right now that Freddy didn't spur enough. He read the bull well and came out of the chute real good, but he rode lazy."

"So he scores better if he rams the bull with his spurs?"

"In this case I'm sure he would have."

We watched two other cowboys position and mind themselves only to get thrown before the eight second whistle. Unlike Freddy's ride, they both were defeated by the bulls unpredictable maneuvers.

Then came Boyd's turn to ride. He drew a bull called Midnight Storm, a black Angus and Brahma cross, which Jeremiah said was also very unpredictable and a lot of spurring wouldn't be necessary. "It would be a major accomplishment just to say on this one," he said.

Boyd went through the typical psyche ritual, which I'm sure any man would need in this type of challenge, and I wondered if Jeremiah's recent scolding effected his concentration. But like his show on the mechanical bull, he squirmed and positioned himself, took several deep breaths, and seemed intently focused.

Pour Some Sugar On Me by Def Leppard played over the loud speaker. After the gate flew open the bull darted straight out of the chute as if powered by a rocket. But Boyd must have anticipated this move because he rode it perfectly—his body anchored to the bull and his free arm stood high above his head. Then the bull twisted and bent his mammoth body as he bucked, creating a ride that in no way compared to anything a mechanical bull could do. Then it spun, like a dog chasing it's tail. But Boyd persisted and the crowd announced their wow with standing applause, which he likely used as fuel to help him last the full eight seconds.

He fell off the bull landing on his hands and knees and stirred a large cloud of dust underneath him. The clowns did a perfect job distracting the bull and lured him away from Boyd and out of the arena. Boyd jumped to his feet, raised his fists and grimaced like a gladiator to the crowd. They cheered him on and when the score came across the board, the announcer called out the large number that flashed in green digitized dots.

"How about a big 93 for the kid from Oklahoma!"

The arena rumbled from the crowd's excitement.

"Wow," I said.

"That was a damned good ride," Jeremiah said.

After a series of exhibitionist type gestures to the crowd, Boyd came back to the chute and eventually looked my way. Though I knew very little about the sport and what was required to accomplish what he had just done, all I had to do was absorb the energy around me to know that it was something spectacular. With that in mind I could do nothing more than offer him a thumbs up and a slight smile.

He slowly nodded back to me, which I hoped was a sign that he knew he'd earned my respect, and that maybe there was no more need for the child's play that had previously taken so much of his energy.

Later in the evening, Jeremiah and I walked through the stock area and I saw Boyd with several other cowboys. By the way he gestured with his hands and body, he appeared to be telling the cowboys about the picture-perfect ride. But when we approached, and they alerted him to our presence, the show stopped and all turned quiet.

"That was a mighty fine ride," Jeremiah said, shaking Boyd's hand.

"Thank ya," Boyd said.

He seemed hesitant at first, but he accepted my hand as well.

"Very impressive," I said.

His face grew firm, as if he were a little uncomfortable. "Appreciate it," he said.

I nodded to him and walked away with Jeremiah, and after a couple steps took a long, deep breath.

"Handled that like a man," Jeremiah said.

"I just had to settle it and this seemed like the perfect time."

"I don't think you've settled anything, yet."

"Why not?"

"He may have made a good ride, and you've probably made it harder for him to continue being an asshole. But there's still the real challenge."

"What's that?"

"Bella."

"Bella? She was my father's woman, for Christ's sake!"

"That don't mean shit. There's more developing between you two than just a friendship and you know it."

The more I thought about it, I supposed he was right. As strange as the situation was, Bella stirred my blood more than any woman ever had. She was talented and beautiful, and unlike Amber, when I held Bella there was something magical in her touch. I suddenly wondered if she felt that way too, or if there had been enough time for her to let go of Jettie and let someone else in. The more I thought about it, I couldn't imagine it being possible. And then there was Boyd. I had never been the type to fight over a woman who wasn't mine in the first place. Boyd seemed to try and stake claim on her as if she were some type of property out for the taking. It's my belief that a woman has a choice in the matter, but apparently Boyd didn't see it that way.

TWENTY

Bella and Boyd went home winners, and both seemed to be at a positive momentum that could help gain enough points to qualify for the National Finals. I had learned that a lot of good things could come to a rodeo athlete who makes the finals. Besides extra income there was the possibility of sponsorship and also endorsements if they placed high enough in the ranks, especially if they became the champion of their event. Neither Bella nor Boyd had ever been there, but it was their goal every year, and this year was as promising as ever.

But what I liked most was seeing Bella smile, which had been minimal since my arrival at Spiro. I was amazed at how much a simple win could put so much spring in her step.

We had camped another night in Hugo and drove home Monday morning. Bella and I both helped Jeremiah unload the livestock and unpack and organize the supplies. This is the part about Rodeo that I assumed most spectators didn't see. All they saw was the contest, the show, and not the continuous rotation of work required to prepare and recover from such a weekend.

Jeremiah parked the Sundowner beside the horse barn and Bella and I unloaded the tack while Jeremiah turned our horses to pasture. She looked very different today, wearing a tan cap rather than a cowboy hat, but her long black hair still flowed out beautifully and tucked behind her ears revealing small studded earrings. She also wore a white T-shirt advertising Justin boots, faded wrangler jeans frayed at the cuffs, and a pair of worn and scuffed work boots. When I entered the barn carrying a saddle she turned and smiled at me offering more of her new spirit.

After laying the saddle on its stand, I turned a large white plastic bucket upside down and sat on it then looked up at her.

"It's real good to see you this way," I said.

"I feel good." She hung a bridle on a hook then looked back at me. "How do you feel?"

"I feel good, too."

"Learn a lot about the rodeo?"

"Yes, I did. And I had a great time."

"That's good."

The tone of our conversation seemed different than any we'd had before, almost awkward. I supposed her new high put her on a different thinking level, and doubted the subject matter at hand was as exciting as the image of the road ahead.

"I want to help you," I said.

"Help me what?"

"You know, make it to the finals."

"I wouldn't know what you could do. It's pretty much just me staying focused, trained, and in good physical shape."

"I can help you with all of those things. If anything, just be here for you, for support."

"That's sweet. But that's not what you're here for. You're here to learn about Jettie."

"There's plenty of time for that, too."

She paused and smiled. "Okay."

I watched her continue to put things away, admiring her in every way. Not just her looks, but also in the way she took care of things. The meticulous way she organized the tack and put it in it's proper place. All that she did was done with so much pride.

"You know," I said, "you have an admirer."

"Oh, who?"

I lowered my voice. "Big, bad, bull-ridin' Boyd!"

She chuckled. "Oh, that's nothing new. He's been chasing me for years. Even when Jettie was around."

"What did he say about it?"

This question seemed to take a little of her high spirit away and I was starting to regret asking.

"He ignored every bit of it. He wasn't the jealous type and he never tried to control me. That's one of the things I liked about him and something that's so difficult to find in men my age."

"That definitely doesn't sound like Boyd."

"No, in fact Boyd is quite the opposite."

"So then I doubt he has much of a chance."

"Chance at what?"

"You know, winning your heart."

"Trevor Hodge, coming from you that offends me!"

"He doesn't seem to want to give up."

"You ought to know that I'm smart enough to avoid guys like Boyd."

"I'd hope so, it's just good to hear you say it."

"And why do you need to hear it?"

"Well, there's something that I'm going to do and I wanted to make sure you understood the real reason why."

"What?"

"Apparently Boyd feels like he's in some sort of competition with me and I'm sure it's over you. I tried to settle it with him, but he doesn't know how to do it my way."

"And what is your way?"

"Well, after his ride I tried to let him know that there was no way I could do what he did, and that he had won whatever competition we had going. Because I knew that in his mind, the prize was you. The way I see it, Boyd is trying to impress you into wanting him for all the wrong reasons. I never try to impress anyone. I follow my own instincts and desires and I just hope I'm liked for who I am."

"That's a pretty good way."

"Then you'll understand that when I do things like ride mechanical bulls, or anything else, I'm not doing it to impress you?"

"I do, but a little showing off doesn't hurt."

"You're not serious, are you?"

She laughed and found another bucket, turned it upside down and sat across from me. "Trevor, there's one thing you have to understand about country girls. When love comes knocking on our door, and we like the man who's doing the knocking, he still has to do his courting."

"Courting?"

"Boyd can ride all the bulls he wants and never impress me. He might earn my respect as a fellow rodeo athlete, but that's about it. All the fancy play he's doing is courting, and it's not working because I don't want him. But if the right guy were to come knocking, all that fancy play is still desired because it's a country boy's way of showing he cares."

"But are you sure you can handle that now? After what happened with Jettie?"

Her face sobered. "I have to admit that you've helped ease a lot of that pain. There's no way I could have rode the way I did at Hugo if it wasn't for what you've brought to me. It's almost like a piece of Jettie has come back to me, only better than before."

"How could it be better?"

"When you put on a cowboy hat and boots, the physical presence is there, but Jettie and I never talked the way you and I do. It's so much better that it keeps me from missing him like I thought I would."

"Well, I'm glad for that. But do you feel like I'm courting you?"

"Are you?"

"I don't know. It's kind of awkward you having been my father's girl, and the fact that he just died no more than two weeks ago, makes it seem almost impossible that you'd be ready for something new."

"You know, there's an old Indian belief that someone dies because someone else is coming, and that certain someone else brings peace with them. I've always believed in that saying, and now I believe it more than ever."

The feelings that swept through me were unlike any I had ever felt before. Thinking of Bella and I as an item was a reverie that I had tried to avoid, mostly because of the common sense that went along with facing the realities in front of me. But not until now did I ever think such a dream could turn out to be real.

She stood and scooted her bucket toward me. As our faces drew closer, I looked into her eyes and absorbed their seriousness. She removed her hat, which released her hair from behind her ears. I touched her cheek with my fingertips and longed to let her know that at this moment there was no place I'd rather be, and no person I'd rather be with. But when our lips met I realized words would be no more convincing. There never was a touch more perfect; a harmonious caress enhanced by the joining of our tongues and desirous exhales of breath. I closed my eyes and allowed myself to be completely free. It was that one unforgettable moment that came without warning and would be forever engraved in my personal history book.

For some reason, possibly out of fear that it may not be real, I opened my eyes to reassure myself. She obviously sensed my lightened passion and opened her eyes as well, looked at me and smiled, then rubbed my cheek with her hand.

"Are you okay?" she asked.

"I've never been better."

She smiled softly then rested her chin on my shoulder and held me in her arms. Suddenly I remembered that I had started to tell her something, and not knowing that we would reach this level of intimacy, I had no idea how to go on. So I decided just to come out with it.

"I want to ride a bull."

I could almost feel her breathing cease, then she backed away from me and gave me a serious stare.

"What are you talking about?"

"I don't think I'll be satisfied until I do."

"Satisfied with what?"

"Knowing who my father really was."

"And how will riding a bull help that?"

"It's more a yearning than anything, but I honestly feel that walking in his shoes would get me closer to an understanding."

"I don't believe this."

"Believe what?"

"You're serious."

"Yes, I am."

She backed away from me, upset the bucket and put her fingers into her hair.

"And that's why I need your support," I said. "As well as Jeremiah's."

She looked at me contemptuously. "One of the things that I liked about you was that you weren't a rodeo nut, and that I didn't have to worry about you getting hurt. And here you are, a greenhorn, with absolutely no idea how dangerous those things are, about to gamble with your life."

"It's not a gamble—"

Tears welled in her eyes and she gritted her teeth. "It's always a goddamn gamble, Trevor! Don't you realize that?"

"Bella, please—"

"No, Trevor. I can't go through it again. So you have to make a choice. Know your father, or know me. It's that simple."

She grabbed her hat and left the barn.

Never had I been so exhilarated one moment, and lost the next. This adventure of mine had me taking some critical and painful, if not unexplained turns. And now I stood at a serious intersection, with a dreadful misery of not knowing where to turn next.

TWENTY-ONE

I hoped to find her somewhere on the ranch, but her Mustang was gone and I had no idea where to start looking. But even if I found her I wouldn't know what to say to make matters better. I couldn't possibly tell her that I wouldn't get on a bull, because I wasn't sure that I could keep that kind of promise. Somehow, I had to convince her that it was just a little something that I had to do, and after I put whatever void there was in my heart behind me, I would give her everything she ever wanted.

Jeremiah came back from the pasture and saw me standing outside the barn. He came toward me in a slow pace, smoldering cigarette hanging from his mouth and face red from the heat. Being that it was not yet noon the day already seemed abnormally hot, and Jeremiah looked as though he'd had enough of it.

"What do you say we get a cold drink," he said.

"All right."

He dropped his cigarette into the gravel and put it out with the toe of his boot, then leaned against the back of his fancy truck still connected to the Sundowner and looked out toward the road. "Where did Bella go in such a tire-squealing rush?"

I leaned on the bed next to him. "I couldn't tell you. But I'm sure it'll be where I can't find her."

"Oh."

I followed him to the deck behind his house where we sat under the table canopy and drank glasses of iced tea that he had requisitioned from Jodie. After a healthy slurp from his glass, he propped both his feet on a chair beside him, tipped back his hat and looked out into the pasture.

I rested both my elbows on the table and nervously thumbed my sweating glass. "I have a favor to ask you."

"Fire away."

"I want to ride a bull."

He gave me a short glance, took another drink then looked back toward the pasture. "Don't sound like no favor to me. Sounds more like a death wish."

"No, if I'm going to do it right, I need your help."

"Yeah, I was afraid you'd say that. Teach a man about fishing and eventually he's going to want to throw a line in the water."

"You had nothing to do with it."

"Ah hell, you wouldn't have known a thing about this place if I hadn't have found you."

"But I'm glad you did."

"Me too, but not if it kills you."

"Then what did you expect me to get from all of this?"

"For the most part, just to learn who your pa was. To claim your inheritance and be comfortable with who you are and where you came from."

"All right. Then what if I couldn't be totally comfortable until I knew what it was like on a bull?"

"You really think there's an answer there?"

"I do."

"Well, I'm not sure I agree with you, but I can't question your reasons. Just you being here has done a lot to help this family heal, especially Bella. And for that I'm damn glad I done it. But if something were to happen to you, if you got hurt, then I'd never forgive myself."

He had a tremendous way of making me feel guilty, but no less adamant about what I felt I had to do. "Then teach me how to do it right. And when it gets down to the wire, when it's time to ride, you make the call."

"What call?"

"If you think I can't do it—that I don't have what it takes to make one ride, then I'll back off. All I'm asking for is one chance, not just to ride a bull, but to really see things from Jettie's point of view."

"You really think I'd do that?"

"I hope you will."

He chuckled a bit. "Trevor, if you have what it takes to ride, and ride only one time, I'll know in less than eight seconds."

"Then you'll help me?"

He paused and studied my stare. "If I don't, you'll probably find somebody else to do it, right?"

"That's right."

"Well then, I reckon since I started this mess, I'd be the one to make sure you get through it alive."

*   *   *

After we had finished putting things away from our weekend, Jeremiah and I drove out to The Oasis. The place was experiencing a normally quiet afternoon, with only a few local ranchers sitting at the bar gabbing with the bartender and drinking Coors Light from longneck bottles.

The bartender greeted Jeremiah by name and retrieved a bottle of Busch Light and brought it to him.

"What'll you have?" he said to me.

"A glass of water would be great."

The bartender gave me a haughty-eyed look then walked away, and returned a few seconds later with a plastic cup full of ice water.

"Can I get you boys anything else?"

"Need to borrow your bull, James," Jeremiah said.

"Go right ahead."

I followed Jeremiah across the dim barroom where he turned the light on above the mechanical bull along with the power to the control panel.

"I thought that the mechanical bull was not a good comparison to the real thing," I said.

"It's not."

"Then why are we training with it?"

"It's good enough to study style and practice form. And right now, that's what we have to work on."

Rather than teach me any technique, he first wanted to see how I naturally reacted to the movement of the bull. He ran a simple pattern of buck and spin, which seemed very minor compared to my ride at The Crossing, and I held right hand up and back straight like Bella had taught me. After eight seconds, Jeremiah stopped the bull.

"You've obviously been studying pretty well."

"I had a little practice at The Crossing."

"You've got the form down pretty good, so let's try it a little faster."

I prepared myself like I had done at The Crossing, shutting everything off around me and thinking "Tilt-A-Whirl". The next ride was closer to the one that night, but still not as rough with the jerks. After the eight-second timer, Jeremiah came out from behind the control panel and stared silently at me.

"What?" I said.

"This ain't good."

"Why ain't it?"

He removed his hat, stared at the floor, scratched his head and exhaled. "Damn, I don't need this."

"Need what?"

"What the hell. I'm going to do this one more time. Tell me when you're ready." Jeremiah held the base of the joystick in the palm of his hand, and the two ranchers at the bar had turned and faced us, as did the bartender, who leaned with his arms straight and his palms on the bar and a white towel thrown over his shoulder.

"All right, I'm ready."

Whatever Jeremiah did with the joystick lever, it created a ride more daring than any I had experienced. After every jerk I felt as though a great force were pulling me off to throw me into the wall. But I held on, my bones jarring and joints popping and everything around me a blur, and after the sound of the whistle, the two ranchers at the bar clapped at hollered.

"Whoa, Jeremiah! Where'd you find that one?"

"Good ride, son!"

As the bull slowed to a stop, Jeremiah ignored the questions, threw down the joystick and carried his beer back to the bar. I climbed down and met him there. He took a large swig from his bottle, then lit a cigarette and looked straight ahead.

"Did I do something wrong?" I asked.

"Hardly."

"So that's good?"

He took another swig and kept staring.

"What's wrong, Jeremiah?"

"Flashback."

"What?"

"The last time I saw a greenhorn ride like that was about thirty years ago, here at the Spiro arena. A sixteen year-old punk climbed up on a real bull for the first time and rode like he'd been doing it all his life. He was a natural."

"Somebody competing against you?"

"No, that punk was my little brother."

I don't know why it took me so long to put two and two together, but when I realized he was talking about Jettie, I instantly understood why it bothered him so much.

"If you can't do this, I understand."

"It's not that. You just caught me off guard. Give me a night to sleep on it and we'll take a bull down to the arena tomorrow afternoon."

"A real bull?"

He looked at me now. "That's what you want, isn't it?"

"Yes, it is."

"I'll take down a bull that's not too rough and that will give you a good feel of the animal. We'll start there."

"All right."

We sat in silence for a moment. I took a drink of my ice water and thought about the main event.

"Jeremiah, what does it require to ride in a real rodeo?"

"An entry fee and a lot of guts."

"That's all?"

"You make it sound like a panty party."

"No, I just figured there'd be more to it."

"That's it."

"Then when I'm ready, I want to ride in a real rodeo."

He took a healthy drag from his cigarette and exhaled the smoke through his nose. "Whatever you want, boy."

"And I want to ride Cyclone."

He gave me a hard stare. "Now that I can't do."

"Why not?"

"Well, for starters, you don't just pick the bull you ride. When you enter a rodeo contest you draw a bull from a lottery."

"Oh."

"And besides that, Cyclone was sold."

"Who'd you sell him to?"

"Contractor down in Midland, Texas."

"What are the chances we could have him brought here?"

He gave me another hard stare. "When will it be enough, Trevor? Don't you realize what we all went through losing your pa? We sold that goddamned bull to rid the horror from our lives. The memory of it is bad enough!"

"I'm sorry. I'm not trying to hurt anyone, I just want you to understand."

"I'll help you, Trevor. But there's limits to how far I'll go."

"Fair enough. You get me to where I can ride, and I'll do the rest."

Now all Jeremiah could do was nod. He finished the last of his beer, put out his cigarette, and said *adios* to the bartender and the ranchers then we left the bar.

Not a word was spoken the entire distance back to the ranch. Maybe I was being selfish to his feelings, and to Bella's, but somehow I couldn't let this fire within me go out. All I could hope for was that some day they would all understand.

TWENTY-TWO

Bella didn't show for our daily workout. I missed her and wished there was something I could do to remedy what had happened. I thought about driving to Poteau to see if she was at the hospital fitness center, but I figured she still needed some time to cool off, and since my mind hadn't changed about what I had to do, I doubted that hers had either.

Jeremiah said he had some business to tend to in Fort Smith, but to meet him at the Spiro arena at three o'clock. So I decided to contact Denny Rose and we agreed to meet for breakfast.

Other than being a rodeo announcer, Denny was also an auctioneer, and every Tuesday auctioned livestock at an auction barn near Sallisaw. The auction barn café was filled with breakfast-eating, coffee-drinking, cowboy hat-wearing cattlemen conversing business and pleasure over their meals. A haze of smoke from the kitchen griddle hovered above the tables and booths, and it carried a mixed scent of bacon, toasted bread, and from the looks of their plates, a variety of other fried meats.

Denny stood from a booth near the back of the café and raised his hand, acknowledging me. He wore a light gray felt cowboy hat and long sleeved white western shirt with a bolo tie. When I arrived at the booth he introduced me to Junior Phelps, owner of the auction barn, who shook my hand, then quickly slammed down the last of his coffee and dismissed himself saying that he had to get to work. But he was polite and said that he admired my father very much.

Denny motioned to the waitress to bring me a menu. A very thin young woman with sandy, shoulder length shag-cut hair came to our booth and handed me a two-sided black and white laminated card the size of a sheet of copy paper. It was badly dog-eared on the corners and the lamination was starting to separate. But it still served its purpose with the breakfast menu on one side and lunch and dinner on the other. As I read down the breakfast side, I nearly laughed at how simple and vague the list was. "One egg .99¢", "Two eggs $1.50", "Additional eggs .25¢ each", and so on. Bacon, ham, or sausage were also available for an additional price, as were pancakes, waffles, oatmeal, and grits. On down the menu was "Omelet $1.99". I asked the waitress what was in the omelet.

"Scrambled egg," she said as she chewed gum.

"Just egg?"

"No, there's other stuff too, but I couldn't tell ya what it was."

"It's good," Denny said, grinning.

"All right, I'll have it."

She scribbled something on a small order pad. "Would ya like anythang to drank?" she asked.

"Just water, please."

"Oh, I wouldn't drank our water, hon." She held her hand beside her mouth and whispered. "Gives everyone the shits."

"O-K. Then how about orange juice? Not made from your water, that is."

She smiled while she chewed, revealing a gold front tooth. "Sure thang, sweetie. Comin' right up."

I handed her back the menu and she walked away. I raised my eyebrows at Denny.

"Nothing like being frank about matters," I said.

He laughed. "She's a good gal. Just lacks a little social polish, that's all."

I grabbed an extra napkin out of a chrome container and the waitress returned with my orange juice. "Hare ya go, hon. Straight from the store-bought jug."

"Thank you."

She winked and smacked her gum and flashed another gold-toothed smile. "Any time, sweetheart. My name's Eileen. Just holler if ya need anythang."

I nodded as she walked away, then cautiously, I took a sip from the glass. It tasted sweet and more like orange punch than real fresh-squeezed orange juice, but it was good, and I'm sure much better than the defiled alternative.

"So how have you been, Trevor?" Denny asked. "Jeremiah treating you fair?"

"He's a good guy."

"Yes, he is."

He took a sip of his coffee and licked his lips. "So what made you decide to come to Oklahoma?"

"I never knew Jettie, and I figured it was now or never."

"Makes sense. Well Jettie was a good old boy, too. I never knew a better bull rider."

"I remember you saying that before. What was so good about him?"

"Natural talent. Not everybody has what it takes to ride them big critters—you know, to have a natural feel for how they move."

"Then why wasn't he ever a champion?"

"Beats me. But if I were to guess, I would say it was something psychological."

"What makes you say that?"

"Well, even Jettie knew he had the talent, but when it came down to pressure, performing in front of the big crowd, he'd lose his concentration. Concentration is all in the mind."

"But you never understood what would make him lose it? The concentration, that is?"

"No idea, pardner."

Eileen showed up with my order and set it in front of me. It was a white oval plate with a tasty looking omelet mixed with onions, tomatoes, green bell peppers and grated cheddar cheese melted on top. She also stood a bottle of Mexican hot sauce beside the plate.

"So how's it look?" she asked.

"It looks very good," I said.

She kept standing with her hands on her hips and looking at me as I unwrapped my silverware from the paper napkin.

"Is there something wrong?" I asked.

"I'm just waiting for you to taste it."

"Oh." I cut a small piece with my fork and put it in my mouth. "Mmm. It's superb."

She grinned and smacked her gum. "I told 'em to cook it special good fer ya."

"Thank you, Eileen. I appreciate it."

"Shore thang, handsome."

She eyeballed me as she walked away. I widened my eyes at Denny.

"You're gonna have to help me sneak out of here."

"Ah, she's harmless. Flirts with all the young fellers."

I poured a dab of hot sauce on the omelet then took another bite.

Denny took a drink of his coffee. "Have you talked to Bella much?"

This question frightened me a little. "Why?"

"She might have the answer you're looking for."

"Bella doesn't know," I said, still chewing. "I'm not sure anyone knows."

"Hell, Jettie may not have even known. It may entirely be a mystery. All I can say is that he had us going for so many years. One year he was predicted by all the experts and critics to go all the way. But at the NFR he flopped, and we all had our hopes so high."

"Did he think he was going to be the champ?"

"Oh, he pretty much ignored all the hype. I'm sure deep down he wanted to be, but I know just the idea of it scared the hell out of him."

As I chewed on another bite of omelet I tried to absorb all that Denny had told me. Everyone informed me that he knew Jettie about as good as anyone, but even he was clueless as to what held the man back. And I wasn't sure the answer, if I knew it, would even help me. And like Denny said, it may always remain a mystery, and we'd have to learn to live without knowing.

"You may think I'm crazy," I said.

"Why's that, son?"

"I'm going to ride a bull."

"You? Why?"

"Not just any bull. I'm going to ride Cyclone."

"Boy, that's nuts. What's the point?"

"I'm not sure I can explain it. It's just something I feel like I need to do."

"Jeremiah know about this?"

"He doesn't like it, but he's agreed to help train me."

"So when is the big event?"

"Don't know. Whenever I'm ready."

"Well, boy, be careful. Cyclone is a tough young bull and there's hardly a bull rider out there who has what it takes to stay on him."

"I'll do my best."

"I'm sure you will, son."

I took the last bite of the omelet, shoved the plate forward and wiped my lips with the napkin.

"One other thing," I said. "Can you think of anyone else that might know what troubled Jettie?"

Denny pushed back his hat, looked down at the table and blew out a large breath of air. "That's a tough one. But you know, you might give Buddy Wells a holler. He worked with your pa a lot in the arena, as a clown. It's a long shot, but he might know something."

Eileen brought the check and laid it on the table, but Denny grabbed it quickly before I had a chance.

He winked. "This one's on me, pardner."

"Thanks."

"Anytime, son. And if you ever need anything, you just give old Denny Rose a holler, you here?"

"I will."

Eileen smiled and stared at me as I left the booth, and Denny left her a couple of one-dollar bills as a tip.

"Y'all come back, now," she said, then pinched me on the back of my thigh. "Especially you, sweet britches."

TWENTY-THREE

J eremiah reached inside a large brown cardboard box and pulled out a folded bundle of leather then tossed it to me.

"What's this?"

"Chaps," he said. "You'll need to wear them."

I unfolded them and let them hang down in front of me. Unlike the handsome and brilliant design I had seen before, these were two, scuffed and worn, long strips of brown cowhide connected by a belt of the same type of leather that went around my waist. They more than covered the front of my legs and fastened on the back with several smaller belts.

Jeremiah explained to me that historically chaps were designed and worn by Mexican *vaqueros* (Spanish for "cowboys") to protect their legs from thorns and cactus needles. "Now days," he said, "chaps are a lot for show, usually custom-made, very fancy and expensive. But they do offer good protection for your legs."

"These don't look fancy," I said.

"That's because they're a real workingman's chaps, and they belonged to your pa."

I studied them closely, and like everything else that had belonged to Jettie—his truck, house, clothing—the chaps were simple and practical. I wouldn't have wanted them any other way.

Jeremiah reached again into the cardboard box and pulled out a black vest, also like what I had seen the cowboys wear at Hugo, and then he handed me a pair of chrome spurs. He showed how to fit the spurs over the heels of my boots, then secure them with miniature belts that wrapped around the front and buckled on one end. These, I had already learned, had a specific use in bull riding, and whichever bull was drawn was the deciding factor on how much they'd be used.

The vest went on like any other and zipped at the front. Jeremiah explained to me how the vest was now mandatory, and that at one time bull riders never wore them. He told me the story of Lane Frost, and how a bull rammed its horn into his ribcage and forced a broken rib into his heart, killing him. "This vest might have saved his life," Jeremiah said.

The thought of a force so powerful helped me realize just how dangerous these bulls really were. All I wore was a long sleeved western shirt, a red plaid from Jettie's wardrobe, which fit in with the profession but nothing to protect any vital organs. Regardless, I held my composure, and the fatal image did nothing to change my mind.

He went on to tell me that the spurs belonged to Jettie, too, but that he never wore a vest.

"Why not?"

"Because when Jettie performed they never thought of wearing such a thing. Not that the idea didn't float around, but somebody had to get killed before it was taken seriously and a cowboy didn't think he was yellow for wearing one."

"If this wasn't Jettie's, then where did you get it?"

"I borrowed it."

"Well, I really don't want to wear it."

"Well, you're going to."

"Jeremiah, if Jettie didn't wear one, then I'm not going to."

"Boy, I think you hit your head on something besides the mat when you fell off that mechanical bull."

"Please, just respect my wishes on this."

"I've been respecting a lot of your damn wishes lately!"

He walked away stern faced and angry, stopped at the back of the trailer, flipped a long steel lever and swung open the tailgate.

The young bull, a yellowish Charbray called Big Banana, seemed overly anxious about the situation. It snorted, the trailer shook as it ran; its hooves beat against the steel floor like large mallets hitting a gong. It darted out into the pen, lowered its head, snorted again and blew a cloud of dust under its chin. Jeremiah climbed over the gate and walked into the pen. The bull looked at him, dug a front hoof into the soil and drug it underneath its brawny shoulders. But Jeremiah quickly opened the gate to the chute, walked around the bull, waved his arms and coerced the animal inside.

I noticed two other young cowboys out in the arena.

"Who are they?" I asked.

"Just a couple local boys. They are going to help save your ass after you get bucked off."

"Oh, like the clowns do."

"That's right."

I studied Jeremiah's face. He appeared upset or concerned, more than he did angry.

"You don't have much confidence in me do you?"

"My confidence don't mean shit, boy. You're the one that needs that."

With all my gear on and ready, minus the vest, I climbed up on the chute fence and looked down on Big Banana's back. By the way the muscles on his shoulders and rump flexed and twitched, I knew he was wound up over the circumstance and all that energy would eventually be released—with me on his back.

Jeremiah draped two devices over the fence; one a long strip of fleece with thick rope on each end, and the other looked like a flat rope with a handle plaited on with strips of leather, and a large bell was also attached midway. He looped the flat rope under the bull's chest and behind its front legs and the bell clanged. The bull jerked and snorted, not seeming to like the object or the noise.

"Now this is the rigging," Jeremiah said. "It's what you hold on to, and once you get on we'll tighten it up and get it to your liking. It shouldn't be too loose, and it shouldn't be too tight, neither."

"What's the bell for?"

"Two things. Most important, it adds weight to the rigging which helps it fall loose when you're done riding, and that helps increase the odds that your hand doesn't get bound up."

"What's the other purpose?"

"The sound of the bell annoys the bull and makes him buck harder."

"Wonderful."

He picked the fleece belt up off the fence. "This is the flank strap or what some call the piss-off belt. We wrap it around the bull's belly in front of his hind legs and it pisses him off."

As high-strung as the animal already seemed, I couldn't imagine that anything else needed to be done to upset him. Nevertheless, Jeremiah strapped on the belt and Big Banana bawled and kicked. I took a deep breath as he put the finishing touches on the piss-off belt and Big Banana tried to fight the whole situation by thumping his massive body against the chute fences and gate, bawling and throwing saliva from his mouth.

"A bull rider has to know the bull before he rides," Jeremiah said. "Big Banana is pretty predictable. He doesn't spin much. He kind of reminds a fella of a big bass that's just been hooked. He'll go straight out of the chute and flex his body to shake off the annoyance, like a hooked bass bends his body when he jumps out of the water. But being a bull, he bucks. So just remember: straight out, bend and buck."

"Do I need to Spur?"

"Boy, you worry about staying on the bull first, then we'll talk about spurring later."

142

I stood on the fence rails above Big Banana and sat down on his back. Like the piss-off belt, he reacted to my position about the same.

"Now remember," Jeremiah said, "use your free hand for balance and don't touch the bull at all with that free hand. And stay forward, don't lean back. Understand?"

I nodded.

The leather glove on my left hand was longer than most, covering all of my wrist and a little of my forearm. Jeremiah helped wrap and tie a narrow strip of leather around my wrist, which he said will help ensure the glove stays on. Then he tightened the rigging while I grabbed the handle with my gloved hand and held on to the fence with my right. With my left palm facing up and under the handle, he laid the rigging rope across it and told me to close my fingers.

"When you let go of the handle that will release the rigging and free your hand."

I nodded.

"Any questions, cowboy?"

I shook my head.

"Nod when you're ready."

Jeremiah climbed down into the arena on the other side of the gate. I looked out at the cowboys in the arena. They were young, probably high school age, and they stood with their hands on their knees waiting for me to come out, but every so often said something to each other and laughed.

I tried to focus, putting my mind on the reason for being here. So I thought about Jettie, his profession and his life, and immediately remembered the importance of staying on this bull.

I looked at Jeremiah and nodded.

He pulled the gate open and Big Banana darted out of the chute just like he had said, bell clanging and all. The sheer power beneath me was almost unfathomable, as if I sat inside a hurricane, everything around me a blur, but I knew that the real storm was below me and not around me. And it was nothing like the mechanical bull. Big Banana bucked, bent its body, and threw its hips left then right, no doubt trying to free itself from the three annoying objects: the bell, the piss-off belt, and me.

Suddenly the bull made a move that tricked every sense of balance I had. It not only caught me off guard, but turned me almost 180 degrees and airborne. There was no time to predict a move, or for thoughts about how to land. There was just gravity and my body pounding into the dirt. Though I seemed to land on all fours, my right wrist caught most of my body weight and bent backward, and a sharp, burning pain traveled through the tendons of my forearm. I looked up and saw the young cowboys dodging the bull, then Jeremiah opened the gate to the stock pen and the bull quickly ran inside.

I clutched my wrist against my abdomen as I stood and looked for my hat. Jeremiah and the two young cowboys came toward me. One of the cowboys found my hat and brought it to me. I was surprised to see Jeremiah smiling.

"You did good," he said, patting me on the back.

"I did?"

"Better than I thought you'd do."

"Nice ride," one of the cowboys said as he reached to shake my hand. I tried but couldn't oblige him.

"You hurt your wrist?" Jeremiah asked.

"I landed on it."

"Let me see it."

I held out my arm, and though it was not sensitive to his touch, it was red and appeared to be swelling behind my hand.

"We better have it checked out," Jeremiah said.

"It's that bad?"

"Always best to get an x-ray to be sure."

He put my hat back on my head, then put his arm around my neck and laughed as we walked toward the gate.

"Why are you so genial all the sudden?"

"I just can't believe you stayed on Big Banana as long as you did."

"Did I make eight seconds?"

"No, more like five."

"And that's good?"

"You expect too much of yourself. That was a good ride for a greenhorn."

"Well I have to do better. Let's get him back in the chute."

"Oh no, that's enough for today. I'm going to take you to the hospital to have that arm looked at."

"Hospital? Jeremiah, I don't need—"

"Trevor, don't argue with me. Besides, you've learned a valuable lesson today about bull riding."

"What lesson?"

"The landing."

"Well it sure wasn't very smooth."

"They rarely are."

"What could I have done different?"

"Probably nothing."

"Then how do I keep from getting hurt?"

"That's the lesson. You don't."

TWENTY-FOUR

I had been waiting almost an hour on an examination table in the Poteau Hospital Emergency Room for a nurse or doctor, or somebody with related importance, to come in and take a look at my wrist. A large plastic curtain that hung from the ceiling and slid inside an aluminum track had been closed around me. So I saw nothing outside of my little area, but heard a little boy outside the curtain whining and crying to his mother about his ankle that apparently, determined from the pinstriped uniform I saw him wearing when I came in, he had injured in a baseball game. Jeremiah had left me alone; said he was hungry and went down to the cafeteria to get something to eat. He asked me if I wanted anything, but my only request was to get this experience over with so I could get back to my training. He had been gone the whole hour.

About fifteen minutes later I heard a voice outside my curtain. It was a familiar voice that spoke sweet to the little boy and said they were taking him to the x-ray room. Then I heard another voice, that of a male, who also talked sweet to the little boy and said he was going to lift him onto the stretcher and take him for a little ride. Suddenly, my curtain opened and Bella stood before me, wearing teal green scrubs, white Reebok athletic shoes, her hair back in a ponytail, and she held a clipboard against her chest.

"Uh, hi," I said.

She didn't smile or say anything. She came inside, turned and closed the curtain back.

"Been waiting long?" she asked, reading from the clipboard.

"No, not really."

"I just came in for a six hour shift. I saw your chart."

"Oh."

"It scared me."

"I'm sorry."

"Are you okay?"

I held out my arm. "I landed on my wrist."

She grabbed a hold of my forearm with one hand and with the other squeezed gently around my wrist. Though the squeeze was supposedly methodical and somewhat painful, I enjoyed feeling her touch again.

"Does that hurt?" she asked.

"Not much."

"Well I doubt there's anything broke, but we should probably take an x-ray just to be sure."

She turned away from me and grabbed the curtain.

"It's good to see you," I said.

She turned her head and looked at me for a short moment, then left my little area without saying a word.

Only a minute or two passed and she came back and opened the curtain all the way.

"Follow me to the x-ray room."

We went into another room where several high-tech mechanisms were mounted on the walls and ceiling and another examination table stood in the middle of the room. She instructed me to sit on a chair and lay my arm up on the table. I laid it on a smooth surface marked with a grid while she pulled down a device suspended from the ceiling. I assumed it was the x-ray camera.

I didn't know what to say to her, but I felt like I needed to say something to settle the tension between us.

"How have you been?" I asked.

"Pretty good. Yourself?"

"Ok, I guess.

She made adjustments to the machine.

"You know," I said, "if you don't want to do this I can wait for another nurse."

She looked at me sternly. "I have to. I'm the only one on duty."

"You're running ER by yourself?"

"The other ER nurse is on break."

"I think she's been on break for over an hour."

"It's called lunch."

"At five o'clock?"

"They still call it that on the evening shift."

"Well, she could have waited until you got here."

"She did. She left you for me on purpose."

"She did? Why?"

"Beats me."

"Oh."

Something told me that Bella had been talking about us, and that possibly her coworker recognized my name when I signed in.

"How'd you hurt your wrist?" she asked.

"On a landing. Given by a bull named Big Banana."

She stopped adjusting the machine. "Big Banana?"

"Yeah, but not eight seconds. Jeremiah said it was about five."

"Is Jeremiah trying to kill you?"

"Why do you say that?"

"Big Banana is a tough bull. Way too tough for a beginner."

"Wow, I didn't know that."

"It's a wonder you only hurt your wrist."

"I guess so."

She slid a cartridge into the x-ray machine and brought it closer to my arm. She told me to spread my fingers apart then draped a heavy vest over my shoulders that hung down over my chest. She left the room and then I heard a brief buzzing sound. She came back into the room and removed the heavy vest.

I couldn't help but look at her. Her smooth, dark complexion. Her silky black hair. She even looked good in the scrubs.

"I really wish there was something I could do."

"About what?"

"I wish I could go back and change things. I liked it better when you were my friend."

"Friend?"

"Well at least that's better than nothing at all. I hate the thought of losing any part of you."

She took a deep breath and looked at the floor for a moment. "I'm sorry if I tried to get too close too quick."

"Me, too."

She raised the x-ray camera and offered me a slight smile. "I'll try to get a doctor to look at this now so you don't have to wait any longer. Meanwhile, you can wait back at that other table. Can I get you anything?"

"You can find that asshole Jeremiah who abandoned me up here."

She laughed. "Okay."

I waited back at my original ER table and a few minutes later an older doctor showed up with Bella. His hair was thick and gray and parted neatly. He wore scrubs underneath a long white coat and a stethoscope hung around his neck. He clipped the x-ray photo on a white board on the wall and flicked on a light switch. The skeletal image of my hand and forearm came into view.

"I hear you've been doing a little bull riding," he said, studying the x-ray.

"That's right."

The doctor now looked at my arm and squeezed it similar to the method Bella had used, only slightly harder.

Jeremiah walked into the room, said hello to Bella then nodded at me. "How you doing?"

"The doctor is about to tell me. Where you been?"

"I'm not much for emergency rooms."

I should have known that places like these probably seemed a little spooky to him, and if nothing else, brought back memories he'd just as soon forget.

"Well, Trevor," the doctor said, "you're lucky here. This is just a sprain."

"That's good," I said.

"How long will it take to heal?" Jeremiah asked.

"Put it in a sling, avoid roughhousing, especially bull riding, and you'll be good as new in six to eight weeks."

Bella raised her eyebrows and I understood that this was something she liked to hear. But Jeremiah winked at me, as though he had some sort of an alternative plan.

The doctor gave me a prescription for some pain medication, said Bella would fix me up with a sling, wished me luck and left the room.

Bella followed the doctor out and Jeremiah came closer to me, leaned forward and whispered. "That's all bullshit, you know?"

"What is?"

"Six to eight weeks. Hell you'll be fit as a fiddle in three."

"Really?"

"Don't pay any attention to that doctor. They exaggerate everything."

Bella returned with a piece of navy blue fabric that she wrapped around my shoulder then slid my arm inside.

"Now, Mr. Hodge," she said, sneering at me. "You do what the doctor says and no roughhousing."

"Yes ma'am."

Then she turned to Jeremiah and shook a finger at him. "And you, too, Mr. Hodge. Behave yourself and keep this cowboy off them bulls."

"Whatever you say, pretty lady."

When she looked back at me, her smile offered more relief than any pain medicine could ever provide. And to see it again, I'd fall off Big Banana a thousand times more.

* * *

On our way back to the arena Jeremiah lit a cigarette, rolled down the pickup window and rested his elbow on the door. He had been so rigid at first, but now seemed almost excited about whatever I had managed to accomplish from the ride, regardless of the minor injury. I wasn't quite sure how to interpret this attitude. It came across as strange and almost uncomfortable.

"I guess I won't be much help on the ranch now," I said.

"Ah, don't worry about that. You're young. You'll heal fast."

"Kind of messes up my training, though."

"Why do you say that?"

"Come on. How am I supposed to train with a strained wrist?"

"Minor setback. In two or three weeks you'll lose that sling and you can get right back on."

"Why this sudden change of heart?"

His quick glance offered the appearance of being caught in a fib. "What are you talking about?"

"Before the ride you were all worried about me getting hurt and fought every desire I had. Now you act as though I'm your next protégé."

He gazed out the window at the passing countryside, exhaled smoke that quickly vanished in the wind. "Maybe you're right. I tend to get a little carried away when I see a young bull rider do a good job."

"Well please don't change. I like it."

"I have to admit, I enjoyed watching you."

"So I did good?"

"For a greenhorn on Big Banana, you did excellent."

I remembered Bella telling me the same thing, and suddenly wondered why he put me on such a tough bull so early in my training.

"Why Big Banana? I thought you were going to put me on an easier bull."

"I thought about it for quite a spell. When Jettie and I were greenhorns, we used to go to a contractor and look over his bull herd and we'd always pick the most challenging bull to practice on. Yesterday when I was riding through the pasture looking at bulls, I couldn't help but feel the same for you. I looked all the bulls over real good, and for some reason the idea of using Big Banana stayed with me and I couldn't let it go."

"I thought you said he was pretty predictable."

"He is. Guaranteed to give you one hell of a ride every time."

"And I rode him good?"

"A lot better than I expected."

"How would it have compared to Cyclone?"

"The difference is that Cyclone is not predictable. Sometimes he bends and sometimes he spins. You just never know what he's going to do."

"Then how does a cowboy prepare for him?"

"That's something that can't be trained. It's a relationship a cowboy has with his own mind that even he may not totally understand."

This was a complicated if not confusing lesson. I was beginning to understand the jargon and physical demands of the sport, but still very ignorant to the mentality required to ride with success. I also wondered if Jeremiah totally understood my quest; that my need for this knowledge was much different than what he and every other cowboy prepared for. It was my own inner resolve; an experience that no one else needed but me. Regardless, now he seemed to be supporting my efforts, and I had to take it any way I could get it.

TWENTY-FIVE

When I woke the next morning my wrist was stiff and sore. I took one of the pain capsules prescribed by the doctor, took a hot shower then dressed in workout shorts and a tank top. For breakfast I prepared a bowl of instant oatmeal and a glass of orange juice. Getting along with only one hand was difficult to get used to, nevertheless, I eventually developed a momentum that worked and found the sling to be a comforting deterrent from using the arm.

I was almost finished with my breakfast when I heard a knock on the front door. Before I got to the door I first thought of Bella, that possibly she had come over for a workout. But when I opened the door she was not the woman who stood before me. It was Jodie, wearing sunglasses and carrying a covered dish.

"Good morning," she said. "I decided to bring a little something for the wounded."

"Oh, thank you. Come in."

I tried to take the dish from her, but with having the use of only one arm she wouldn't allow it, and took it to the kitchen herself. She sat it on the kitchen table then removed her sunglasses.

"Do you like Mexican casserole?"

"I've never had it."

"It's nothing fancy. Just some refried beans, ground beef, cheese, tortilla chips, and a little sour cream on top."

"It sounds good."

"And you can add some jalapenos and salsa if you like."

"I might do that."

"So how are you feeling today?"

"A little sore, otherwise fine."

She walked out of the kitchen and peered into each of the rooms. "I like what you've done to the place."

"Oh, I haven't really done anything. Bella is the one that did the cleaning."

Jodie looked back at me and delivered a slight smile. "So how is she doing?"

I shrugged. "I can't be sure. She's difficult to figure out."

"Yes, she is."

The humidity was on the rise and the house felt stuffy, so I invited Jodie outdoors where there was at least a warm breeze. We walked through the front yard while above us several sparrows chirped in the maple trees and a blue jay squawked and jumped from limb to limb.

"I guess you can say that your stay here has been eventful," Jodie said.

"Very much so."

"Are you planning to get on a bull again?"

"Yes, I am."

"I see."

"You sound as though you don't agree with it."

"Doesn't matter, does it? It's your decision."

"Yeah, but I'd like your opinion."

"I try to avoid judging other people's lives. Only they know why they do what they do. Just like I'm sure you have your reasons."

"I wish everyone were as understanding as you."

"I don't think it has much to do with understanding. It's more like trying not to be overly concerned or too selfish."

"Why do you say that?"

"We're all concerned about you, Trevor. You were a lost loved one who has come home, and what you're doing is dangerous. We don't want to lose you again."

I didn't quite know how to respond. What she said was touching, and didn't at all seem selfish. "I'm really grateful for Jeremiah finding me and introducing me to all of you. But more than anything, I'm grateful for the opportunity to learn who my father really was."

"But you see, if you get hurt, then Jeremiah will feel guilty for finding you. And I want you to understand that."

"I don't mean to put that kind of pressure on him, or Bella, or you, or anyone. I just feel that my real loss was never knowing my father. Sure, I've got to know all of you, but until I know Jettie, I don't think I'll ever be satisfied."

Jodie stopped walking and I followed suit. She faced me and grabbed my hand and held it between both of hers. "Maybe that's where we're a little selfish."

"How?"

"Because you have a good reason for doing what you're doing, and we're trying to give you reasons why you shouldn't."

"So you think it's a good reason?"

"If I were in your shoes, I'd probably do the same thing."

"It feels real good to hear you say that."

She hugged me and kissed my cheek, then looked into my eyes. "And you hang in there with Bella. One day she'll understand."

"I look forward to that day."

After Jodie left I decided to get started with my workout. Being somewhat handicapped I knew I wouldn't be able to do a lot, but I wanted to at least keep my legs and abdominals in shape, and possible a few curls with my good arm. I got down on my knees and reached under the bed with my good hand and found the vinyl workout mat, but I couldn't reach either of the dumbbells. I leaned to my side and looked under the bed and found them. I grabbed one and saw a red shoebox far to the other side. I had never noticed the shoebox before, but figured I had never looked that far under the bed before. So I walked around to the other side and reached underneath and pulled out the box. It was dusty, but looked as though it had recently been touched. I removed the lid to find several letters like the one Jeremiah had given me when I came down for the funeral. I remembered him telling me that there were more letters, which explained why the box looked as though it had recently been opened.

I counted fourteen letters, all identical to the one I had already read, other than the dates on the postmarks. The date span ranged from December to April. None had been opened and all were stamped "return to sender".

I arranged them in order by date and opened the earliest one, postmarked December 20, 1977.

December 19, 1977

My dearest Bonnie,
You've been gone over a month now and I keep wondering whether you are going to be home for Christmas. Jodie said she heard you'd moved to Kansas City and I had to go to quite a bit of trouble to find you. I figured you'd be staying with that old girlfriend from Sallisaw who moved up there to work for that greeting card company. I was surprised to find out that you had rented a house and got a job there too. Bonnie whatever I've done to run you off I wish you'd forgive me and come home. I sure do miss you and little Trevor. I bought him a little toy tractor for Christmas. It looks just like mine and I figured he'd like that. I don't know what else to say other than I can't imagine spending Christmas without you and my boy. Please come home, Bonnie. I love you. And tell Trevor I love him too.

All my love,
Jettie

The letter was hard to read. He seemed abandoned, hopeless, and almost pitiful. And to think that the letters were returned and never read, made me wonder if things would have been different if Mom would have read them.

I kept opening letters and reading them. It was more of the same; only the tone steadily grew worse, as if in desperation, giving up on life and getting used to nights alone, passing out under the influence of corn whiskey.

Then came the last letter, postmarked April 10, 1978. Different than the others, the edges of the envelope were covered with clear cellophane tape that had browned over the years.

April 10, 1978

Dear Bonnie,

All your letters have come back now so I guess it's very unlikely you'll read this one. Maybe I'm just writing it for myself. All I know is that I've done all I can to win you back. My trip to Kansas City almost landed me in jail, only because I wanted to see my little boy and give him his Christmas present. I guess that really proved how you felt about me. I've come to grips with that now and I guess I'll just have to let it go. It's been so long since I've seen little Trevor that I wonder if I'd even recognize him. I'm sure he's grown like a prairie weed. I wonder if he'd even know me. I guess I'll just have to hope that you raise him good because without you Bonnie I don't see how I could ever be a good daddy. Being gone all the time is no life for a little boy. So maybe its just best that I stay out of his life and let you raise him the best you can. And one day I hope you'll tell him that his daddy loves him, and that some day maybe he could come down and go fishing or to a rodeo and watch the bulls. I'd sure like that someday. Please give Trevor the package taped to this letter and tell him it's a special present. You don't have to tell him who it's from.

All my love,
Jettie

A ton of emotion welled up inside me. Some of it anger, but most was sadness. I wanted to cry but couldn't. The image of him visiting our house haunted me. All he wanted was to see his little boy, his own flesh and blood, and give him his Christmas present. And I saw the image of a Massey Ferguson replica, a tiny rendition of something real to help remind the little boy of who his father was and how he lived. The entire image made me want to drive to Kansas City and force my mom to read all these letters, explain to me how she could avoid a man with so much love, and also so much pain. I couldn't understand any of it. More than ever I needed answers—answers that I would search endlessly to find, no matter how difficult the journey might be.

I knew that eventually most of those answers would have to come from my mom. But by avoiding him, she purposely kept herself from knowing what was in his heart. The letters proved how much he loved me then, but they didn't explain the rest of his life. Why didn't he go on and find another love? Why didn't he become the best damn bull rider there ever was? Suddenly I remembered my conversation with Denny Rose, and without much hesitation found the phone book and located the number. Tonight seemed like a perfect night to do some fishing.

TWENTY-SIX

T he full moon cast a healthy glow over the calm surface of the Arkansas River, and it highlighted the tops of the trees on the opposite bank, as though they were outlined by a white neon light. It shined down on our fishing lines and, where the line entered the water, accented the ripples created by the underwater currents that shifted the position of the lines. And it shined down on our faces, so much that I could make out the details of Buddy's profile and the Coors Light label on his beer bottle as he slumped in a lawn chair and tipped the bottle to his lips.

We fished for catfish, either flathead or channel cat, as heavy as twenty pounds. We used beef liver for bait, bound on the prongs of a treble hook and releasing a stench that Buddy said the catfish liked. We monitored two poles each, which were equipped with open-faced reels. The reels were wound with strong nylon line weighted with lead sinkers and tossed in four different directions. Apparently Buddy thought nothing of my handicap, as I knew that if I hooked a "twenty-pounder" there was no way I could reel it in. But he told me not to fret, to hook the fish first then we'll worry about bringing it in.

Though the idea of catching a really big fish was somewhat enthralling, it was not at the peak of my interest. I relaxed in my own lawn chair and enjoyed the serenity of the evening, the cold beer, and occasionally the quiet conversation that was usually prompted by a cry of some sort of nocturnal being, which thus far Buddy had identified as being from either a coyote, a screech owl, or a whippoorwill.

"I can see why Jettie liked this. It's very relaxing."

"Jettie could have cared less if he ever caught a fish. All he wanted was the night air."

"Did you guys fish a lot together?"

"At first it was once a week, between rodeos. But after I retired, we hit the river more often."

"What was it like in the old days, when you worked with Jettie in the arena?"

This made him smile. "Them was the best years of my life. I was almost thirty years old when I first met Jettie. He was a greenhorn bull rider and my glory days were behind me. That's when I started working as a clown."

"You were a bull rider, too?"

"That's right. Even qualified for national finals once."

"Wow. So what made you decide to be a clown?"

"I was asked by a fella down in Mesquite. I knew I couldn't ride no more, and it beat working at some factory. Besides that, I knew bulls and knew how to play them. So the job fit me real well."

"So you were a clown when Jettie rode?"

"Yessir. The first time Jettie came out of the chute at a PRCA event, I was in the arena. He made a good ride, too. Eight seconds and scored a ninety-one. I'll never forget it. But it wasn't the ride that made it so memorable. He spurred the hell out of that bull, and when he jumped off, that bull spun and came right after him. There wasn't a clown in this country that could have lured it away."

"What happened?"

"I put myself between Jettie and the bull and caught a head butt in the ass. We were close to the fence and Jettie made the climb, but I was on the ground. The other clown came to help and slapped the bull on the rump just before he was about to rip my guts out. Lucky for me, the bull decided to go after the other clown and he lured it out of the arena. Jettie climbed down and asked me if I was all right. He helped me up and I limped out of the arena. I sure was sore the next day. Yeah, I thought I'd had friends before, but I never knew what true friendship was until I met Jettie."

"What made him such a good friend?"

"We understood each other. He was a professional and very mature for his age. He didn't fart around and took everything about the profession seriously."

"I've been told he was good."

"One of the best."

"Then why wasn't he a champion?"

"That's a good question, pardner. I've been right there in the arena and watched him for years and never seen anybody ride better. But something always happened to him at the finals. When he got on a bull he wasn't the Jettie Hodge we all knew."

"No idea why?"

"My guess was that it was something very personal. We were good friends, but I never had the guts to pry."

I felt as though I had hit another dry well. Like Bella, Denny, or even Jeremiah, Buddy couldn't provide me with the answers I wanted. They all claimed it was private, psychological, locked up inside of Jettie like a curse. But some inner voice told me the answer was out there, and that I had to keep searching, and that possibly if I looked hard enough I'd start finding clues.

"Did you ever do anything else together besides fishing?"

"Sometimes we'd go to his house and cook steaks on the grill and drink hot toddies."

"Hot what?"

"Toddies. Whiskey and hot water."

"Is that good?"

"It's a good drunk!"

The image of Jettie being drunk made me think again of the dare. I wasn't quite sure how to ask, but I wanted to hear what Buddy knew.

"I was told you were there when Jettie was killed."

He looked at me, half his face shadowed by the darkness, the other half highlighted by the moon and revealing a blank expression.

"I was there," he said.

"I'd like you to tell me about it—if you can."

He looked back toward the river, then up at the moon. He tipped his beer bottle up high, gulped down its contents, then tossed it into a pile of other bottles and opened another.

"It all started at a place called Billy Bob's, a big club down in Fort Worth. You have to know that Jettie didn't go to clubs very often. For some reason that night he had a party itch. We'd been there a couple of hours when a group of young cowboys came to our table. They were Oklahoma boys we'd known for years. At first they were all friendly-like, complimenting Jettie on his history and talents, and buying him drinks. After about four shots of tequila, which mixed with the four or five beers he'd already had, they started poking at his nerves."

Buddy paused and took a swig of beer.

"What about?" I asked.

"Bella."

"Bella?"

"I remember one of them saying, 'So tell me, Jettie, how does an old man like you keep a young Indian princess like that happy?' Jettie rarely got riled over such talk. But the tequila took all his good sense away."

"What'd he do?"

"Like a drunken fool he squabbled with them."

"What did he say?"

"He said that he could do anything them young punks could do. And one of them said, 'Yeah, but your bull ridin' days are

162

long gone.' And that was the wrong thing to say to Jettie Hodge, drunk or not."

"So this is when they went to the arena?"

"Almost. They bickered a while longer, when finally Boyd said, 'Hell man, if you still got the stuff then prove it.'"

"Wait a minute. Who'd you say?"

"Boyd. Boyd Simmons. He's a local—"

"Yeah, I'm familiar with Boyd. He's the one who dared Jettie?"

"Yeah, he instigated most of it. He's had this thing for Bella for quite some time and getting Jettie riled was his way of trying to make Jettie look bad."

"Getting him killed was a sure way of doing that. Didn't any of you try to stop him?"

"I did, but I was grossly outnumbered. Boyd and his boys held me back. Boyd even shoved me once. 'Stay out of it, clown!' he said."

This bit of news made me very angry. I had tried to keep myself from disliking Boyd, though his tactics were crude, if not totally juvenile, and I had tried to be friends with him. But any man who had the audacity to provoke a drunken man to do something so dangerous was obviously a man with no conscious.

"Did anyone ever confront Boyd about it?"

Buddy took a drink of beer then shook his head.

"Why not?"

"Because it was a foolish prank that got out of hand. This sort of thing happens every now and then and you just have to deal with it."

"Deal with it? Hell, I would have pressed charges! Maybe even had it investigated by the police, encourage the prosecuting attorney to bring up charges of manslaughter or something."

"You act as though Boyd wanted your pa to die."

"Well, he sure wanted him out of the picture as far as Bella was concerned. And he got his wish, didn't he?"

"But it didn't work, did it?"

"Buddy, Jettie is dead."

He tipped his bottle up and drank the last of its contents then stood from his chair and angrily threw the bottle into the river. The bottle splashed into the water and reflected an amber glow from the moonlight as it bobbed up and down in the slow current. Suddenly one of my lines pulled tight and moved to the left, and the fiberglass fishing rod bent with it.

"I think I've got something," I said.

Buddy rushed to the pole, picked it up and turned the reel lever. He turned it slowly but persistently, letting out an occasional grunt.

"This feels like a hog," he said.

The line was almost at a 90-degree angle from the base of the pole, and Buddy walked the edge of the bank following the direction of the pull.

"Get ready, Trevor! She's a monster!"

I stood next to the water waiting for the image of this monster to appear. I would be lying if I said I wasn't a bit scared. Sure, it was just a fish. But one that desired smelly beef liver—a hog, a monster. How was a greenhorn like me supposed to feel?"

Suddenly their was a sharp piercing sound and the line disappeared.

"Ah, hell!" Buddy said.

"What happened?"

"That heavy bastard broke the goddamn line."

"Must have been real big then, huh?"

Along with the fishing pole that dangled a curled and broken line, Buddy moped back to his chair, dropped the pole to the ground then opened another beer. He took several swallows and after that didn't say a word.

"Oh well," I said. "We've got three more poles. Let's see that fat hog try it again."

He looked up at me and eventually laughed. I laughed with him, sat in my chair and opened a fresh beer for myself.

TWENTY-SEVEN

Mesquite, Texas was famous for its championship rodeo and a place Jeremiah visited frequently, never as a contractor, but as a spectator on free weekends. He still brought his Sundowner trailer and rode in the grand entry, but mostly it was a moment where he enjoyed a stress free period of simply observing other stock and laughing and sharing stories with old friends. Bella, however, was a barrel race participant, and since Jeremiah and Jettie had always traveled together to Mesquite, she had arranged her schedule to be there at the same time. For me it was more than just another rodeo experience, I figured it was an opportune time to confront both of them at once.

Inside the front of the Sundowner, Jeremiah sat in a soft cushioned chair with his feet propped up, enjoying a cold bottle of Busch Light and telling me a story about a one-armed bull rider he once knew named Charlie Baird. Being that my arm was in a sling, I guess he thought the story was somewhat appropriate. He said that the boy got his wrist caught in a piece of farm machinery, and they ended up having to amputate it up to the elbow.

"How'd he keep his balance?" I asked.

"He strapped on a prosthetic limb. Looked like a hand and forearm off a mannequin down at the J. C. Penney store."

"Did it work for him?"

Jeremiah couldn't finish the story without laughing.

"Sometimes it did," he said between gasps. "But one time old Charlie got on a real spinner, and his arm got to flipping back and forth so hard that the limb fell clean off and hit one of the clowns upside the head."

He had me laughing now.

He went on to tell me about the knot that swelled on the clown's head, and that's when Bella opened the door and stepped inside. We were still laughing, but I quickly poised myself.

"Jodie said you wanted to see me," she said.

"That's right," I said.

She straddled a bench seat near the door and put her palms on her knees. She wore a white-laced western shirt, a white straw hat, and dark blue Lawman jeans. Jeremiah was still chuckling and she asked what was so funny.

"He told me the story about one-armed Charlie. Ever heard it?"

She rolled her eyes. "A thousand times."

Jeremiah grabbed another beer out of the miniature refrigerator and offered us each one. We both declined.

"So what's on your mind?" Bella asked, looking at me.

"I have something I need to ask the both of you, and it's very important that I get an honest and sincere answer."

"That's the only way I operate," Jeremiah said.

"Last night I went fishing with Buddy. He told me more about the night Jettie was killed, specifically what happened at the bar."

Jeremiah's face was still red, but they looked at each other gravely.

"Why didn't you guys tell me it was Boyd?"

Bella crossed her arms over her chest, exhaled and slouched slightly. Jeremiah leaned forward and thumbed at his beer bottle.

"I'm sorry, Trevor," Jeremiah said. "Especially if you thought we was keeping it from you."

"You were," I said matter-of-factly.

"We just didn't want you doing anything foolish," Bella said.

"Let's not talk about doing anything foolish. Let's talk about holding Boyd legally responsible for what he's done."

"We thought about that," Jeremiah said. "But truthfully, Boyd was just being the stupid redneck he is and we really don't think he intended to hurt Jettie."

I looked at Bella. "Do you believe that?"

She shrugged. "I don't know, Trevor."

"Well I think it's all bullshit. You both know that it's all some country boy courting thing with old-fashioned consequences. Why would anybody entice a drunken man to get on a bull? It makes no sense unless you're a cruel man with no conscience or a man after something. Well I think Boyd is both, and the proof lies in his past and present actions. Was he at Jettie's funeral? Has he ever offered the family his condolences?"

They remained silent.

"I didn't think so."

"So what do you want to do?" Bella asked.

"First I want an explanation."

"What kind of explanation?" Jeremiah asked.

"Why you and everyone else were so passive about it."

"What did you expect us to do? This is cowboy country, Trevor. Believe me, I've been around it all my life and this sort of thing happens all the time."

"Then where is your need for a cowboy style of justice, Jeremiah? For Christ's sake your brother was killed! All because of some stupid dare that we all know was somewhat intentional. Please explain to me why nothing was done."

"Well the law is tough around here," he said. "Unless you're friends with the law or related to them in some way, then it's tough to get the kind of justice you're talking about. I'm no friend of our sheriff, and I'm not related neither. But Boyd so happens to be his nephew."

"His nephew?"

"That's right. And if we brought charges against Boyd, it would mean hell for all of us."

"You're kidding."

"No I'm not."

"So you're saying that nothing can be done?"

"My daddy—your granddaddy—used to say that we should deal with folks in the kindest way we can, and for those whom we can't deal with, we leave to the hands of God."

"I see, and what has God done so far?"

"That's not for us to question."

"The hell it's not. God helps those who help themselves. My other granddaddy said that."

Bella stood up and put her hands on her hips. "Okay, guys. Let's not argue over this. Jeremiah, in the beginning I felt like you did, but now I'm a little more like Trevor and I'm afraid he might get hurt. I don't think it's going to stop unless we put a stop to it."

Jeremiah exhaled and leaned back in his chair. "All right. What do you want to do?"

"Boyd has paid entry fees for here tonight, right?" I asked.

"That's right," Jeremiah said.

"Tonight I want us all to go over to Billy Bob's in Fort Worth, and Bella, I want you to lure Boyd there."

"I can do that," she said.

"Have him meet you there. Sit down with him and start ordering him shots. We'll be at a table not far away so you don't have to worry about anything."

"What are you going to do?"

I seemed lost for the word. "What is it when you fire a gun and the bullet hits something and comes back at you?"

"Ricochet?" Jeremiah said.

"That's right," I said smiling. "Ricochet."

TWENTY-EIGHT

oyd took second place at the Mesquite Rodeo and it was the perfect situation for Bella to offer him a chance to celebrate. I watched them come in at Billy Bob's. She hung on his arm and played the plan superbly. They took a table near a staged area where a band called Ghost Town Council performed, singing a song called "That's Cowboy." A waitress brought them a tray of tequila shots and Boyd acted surprised but he quickly slammed two down and chased them with beer. After a big swallow of brew he raised his hand and yelled at the band. One of the singers, dressed authentic cowboy with a thick and neatly groomed mustache pointed back at Boyd and accentuated a few words of the song. "That's cowboy, and that's the life for me!" Boyd raised his beer bottle and yelled again then kissed Bella. When he looked back at the band she glanced at me and scowled as though she'd just tasted sour milk. I felt a little sorry for her, but at least the music was good.

Jeremiah and I had watched them for several minutes when we noticed Buddy walk in with two other guys, big chesty boys who were old friends of both Buddy and Jettie. They took a table not far from Bella and Boyd and a waitress brought them each a bottle of Lonestar beer.

Bella had been ordering the shots in doubles, and Boyd took them both and each time chased them with beer. He had now had six shots altogether, and after that sixth chaser, I looked at Jeremiah and smiled. He grinned and shook his head.

"He'll be jelly if we don't act pretty soon."

Just as we were about to get up Boyd stood from the table and staggered toward us. For a moment I thought he was coming to talk to us but I quickly realized he headed for the urinals. Just before he got to the entrance, he noticed us and staggered to us.

"Well, lookee there," he said. "There's the little old Hodge boy. What did you do to your wrist, Hodge boy? Hurt yourself whacking off?"

He nearly fell over from laughing at his own joke.

"No, it happened when your sister tied my arms to the bed post. She said you liked it that way, too."

He returned a befuddled frown then came at me but Jeremiah quickly interjected.

"Go take your piss, Boyd," Jeremiah said.

He backed away slowly and eventually smiled. "Yeah, you talk tough. But look yonder over there." He pointed at Bella. "She wanted to party with a real cowboy tonight."

He walked away laughing and staggering. After he went into the men's room we left the table and joined Bella. And when he came out and saw us sitting at the table with Bella his eyes lit up like street lanterns. He worked his way through the crowd and when he arrived at the table he looked down at me, then at Jeremiah.

"What the hell do you all want," he said.

"Sit down, Boyd," I said. "I want to talk to you."

"Well I don't want to talk to you, city boy. So git!"

"You have no choice in the matter."

"What?"

I glanced at Buddy and his boys and Boyd followed my gaze. One of Buddy's friends glared back at Boyd and pointed his finger in a downward gesture. When Boyd looked back at me I told him again to sit down. He sat.

"What the hell do you want?"

The waitress came and set another shot in front of Boyd.

"Drink up, cowboy," I said.

He glanced wearily at the shot then at Bella, who appeared to be having great difficulty keeping a strait face.

"What are y'all up to?" he asked.

"You're a tough guy, Boyd. You can handle it."

He took the shot and swallowed and shuddered a bit, then along with a little muscular and eye-ball intimidation from Buddy's friends, we coaxed Boyd to the parking lot where he climbed into the cab of a pickup and sat between the two big boys. Buddy, Bella and I joined Jeremiah in his extended cab that pulled a stock trailer and led the way to that fateful arena.

Boyd likely was beginning to get the picture, as he struggled with the two men that drug him by the arms to the bucking chute area. Jeremiah opened the tailgate to the trailer and a snorting, salivating black Brahma stormed out into the chute.

Boyd's eyes were as wide as silver dollars. He started screaming and hollering as they lifted him above the chute where he could look down over the bull's back. He wriggled and tried to get loose but the boys held him tight by the arms. Bella came forward with a black rubber bucket full of water, climbed up on the fence and tossed the contents into Boyd's face. The force of the water pushed his hat from his head and he gasped and choked as some of the water had gone inside his gaping mouth.

I climbed up the fence next to Bella. "Sorry we had to get you so drunk," I said wryly.

"I'll kill every damned one of you!"

"Just like you killed Jettie?"

His wet hair fell over his eyes and he grimaced and spat. "You go to hell!"

I looked down at the bull that sat amazingly still during all the commotion. "You know, Boyd's a pretty good bull rider, so maybe we better get Mr. Brahma a little more riled."

Jeremiah came forward with the flank strap and rigging and put them on the bull, which instigated the typical bull-in-the-chute type objections.

"I think I'll tighten the flank strap a little tighter than normal," Jeremiah said.

"Did you give him some of that good high-energy grain?" I asked.

Jeremiah winked. "Just enough to make him real spicy."

"And how about the rigging bell?"

"Gave the clapper a shot of WD-40. It'll be extra noisy and much more annoying."

"Excellent. So what do you think, Boyd? They say this Brahma is a real spinner. Up for it?"

He squirmed, cussed and kicked but the boys had a good hold on him. Jeremiah rammed a cattle prod against the bull's rump and it liked to kick the chute apart. Boyd screamed.

"I don't understand, Boyd. I thought you was a tough cowboy."

"All right," he said. "Stop this shit and tell me what you want."

"I want to see you ride. You seem to take a keen liking to watching cowboys ride drunk so I want to see for myself what's so damned fascinating about it."

"All right. I'm sorry. Is that what you want to hear?"

"Sorry? I don't think so. Boys, on the count of three, Jeremiah will open the gate and you drop Boyd on the bull."

Jeremiah handed Bella the cattle prod and stepped down in front of the gate.

"One—"

"Wait! I didn't mean for Jettie to get killed. Honest!"

"Oh really. What did you expect?"

"Hell, I don't know. I was just having some fun."

I gritted my teeth. "Well your fun killed my father, you son of a bitch!"

"Trevor, no—"

"Two!"

"Please, stop!"

Bella stuck the bull with the cattle prod again.

"Three!"

Jeremiah pulled the gate open and the boys dropped Boyd onto the bull's back but held on to his arms. He screamed and cried as the bull ran out from underneath him and bucked and kicked into the arena. We all laughed.

"You bastards!" Boyd said.

"Now that's a fine attitude," I said. "Jeremiah, get the bull back in here."

"No!" Boyd cried. "I mean it! I'm really sorry and I'll make it up to you!"

"All right, let's talk business. What are you willing to do?"

"Whatever you want."

"For starters I want your assurance that you'll not tell a soul about what happened here tonight. Especially your legal connections back in Spiro."

"You have my word."

"Second, you work for Jeremiah and I for thirty days on the ranch, doing anything we want. Free labor, so to speak."

"Free labor?"

"Hey, we can always bring the bull back in."

"No, no. All right. I'll do it."

I patted him on the shoulder. You're a good man, Boyd."

They let him down and he stumbled out of the chute and into the arena, falling on his face. We all laughed when he stood—his wet head mixed with the arena dirt making mud, and his eyes wide as the Brahma squalled and came charging toward him. For a drunken cowboy, he climbed a fence pretty good.

TWENTY-NINE

I took off my sweaty work clothes and climbed into the shower. The warm streams of water soothed my labored muscles—the result of a long and hot day on the ranch. Along with Boyd (our new temporary hand) we had helped Jeremiah get stock ready for a junior rodeo competition to take place in a couple of days. So far Boyd had lived up to his agreement in good fashion. He did as he was told and didn't gripe. But it's not like we treated him as a slave. The way we saw it, the best way to make us feel better about Boyd was to make him feel better about himself. He was a talented bull rider, and of course he already knew that, but Jeremiah explained to him that the gifts in this world are not what you receive, but what you give to others. He said that Boyd needed nothing more than to get his head on straight and experience some of the good things in life. We figured that helping young kids would be a good test for him, plus our own version of a modern-day attitude remedy.

After drying myself off I wrapped the towel around my waist and went to the bedroom to get dressed. I sat down on the edge of the bed wondering what to wear and how to spend the evening. I was bone tired and figured a night at home in the little bungalow would be good for a change. So I changed into a pair of boxer shorts and a T-shirt, grabbed a beer and headed for the davenport. I thought about turning on the television, but I noticed several thin paperback novels in a wooden magazine rack near the end of the davenport. I started looking through them. All were westerns of various titles and authors, but one in particular caught my attention: *The Good Old Boys* by Elmer Kelton.

I leaned back on the davenport, turned on the three-way lamp above me, opened the cover of the book and read an inscription.

> To Jettie Hodge
> Best Wishes
> Elmer Kelton
> Austin, Texas 1980

I started reading and became absorbed in the story. I'm not sure how much time had passed but I had read more than half of the novel, and I laid my head back on the arm of the davenport thinking of one of the scenes where the main character in the story helped his nephew raise a windmill tower. It was a scene I could easily relate to, but only because of this time in my life and the relationship I had built with Jeremiah.

Sometime during that thought I drifted to sleep, and found myself facing, once again, the applauding crowd. This time, however, I was not outside my office cubicle, but under the bright sunshine at the Spiro arena. I recognized everyone now; Denny, Buddy in clown gear, the young cowboys from the day I rode Big Banana, the big cowboys from Billy Bob's, the members of Ghost Town Council, pregnant Tanya from Barney's, and even gum-chewing Eileen from the sale barn café. The one person missing was Walter, but in his place was Boyd, standing with arms crossed and not applauding. Then I heard the eight-second whistle, only to wake moments later from the sound of a ringing telephone. I rose quickly and reached for the phone at the other end of the davenport. I answered with a dry, raspy voice.

There was a short hesitation on the other end of the line, but when she finally said my name the voice seemed almost foreign.

"Mom?"

"Were you asleep?"

"Uh, just taking a little nap. How are you?"

"Doing fine, but wondering a lot about you."

I looked down at my wrist, which felt a little stiff, and worked my fingers into a fist. "I'm doing pretty good."

"I assume since you haven't come home that you're enjoying yourself?"

"I am. Learning a lot about rodeo and ranching. Jeremiah and Jodie are great."

"I see."

"So how are things with Walter?"

"Oh, Walter and I had a little disagreement."

"No way."

"Yes, I know you thought we were the perfect couple. But things just didn't seem to work out."

"Maybe you're just destined to be an old spinster."

"Don't say that."

"No really, maybe I should buy you a little short-legged dog that barks at every little noise. You know, one of them Chihuahua's or Pugs, or something like that. You can spoil him—overfeed him and make him fat and live happily ever after."

"Trevor, you're being mean."

"I know. I'm sorry."

"No you're not. You meant every word of it."

"I just think you make poor choices, Mom. Why don't you quit dating guys for what they do and fall in love with somebody for who they are?"

"Tried that. It didn't work."

"With who?"

"I'm sure you don't remember. You were just a baby."

"Then why don't you tell me about it."

"Surly there's a better time."

"No, now is a perfect time."

There was a short pause, then she took a deep breath. "His name was Darrin. He was from Sallisaw."

"How did you meet a guy from Sallisaw when you were in Kansas City?"

"I wasn't in Kansas City yet, Trevor."

"Oh."

I'd known Darrin for quite a long time, but he and this other girl had gone together for years. Went to the prom together, and eventually got engaged. Plus, I was with Jettie and things never seemed to be right. But we always made eyes at each other."

"But you were together?"

"He got married a little before Jettie and I did. And you came along not long after that. I was extremely unhappy and so was he. We ran into each other one day in Fort Smith. We decided to have lunch and that's how it all started."

"How what started?"

"The affair."

"So you didn't just leave Jettie? There was someone else?"

"That's right. He left his wife and we ran off to Kansas City together."

"What was so special about this guy?"

"I don't know, there was just something about him I had always liked. He wasn't a cowboy, for one. He ran a construction business and he had this opportunity to take on a big job in Kansas City. So we left."

"And you were in love with him?"

"Yes. I loved him."

"So what happened?"

"We were together for less than a year. I had divorced Jettie and he had divorced his wife. But I don't think he could ever get used to you. You weren't his child and he was jealous of Jettie. That alone created a huge problem for us."

"So why did you break up?"

"One day we had this huge fight. The next thing I knew he was seeing his old wife again. He went back to her and it all came to an abrupt end."

"Wow."

"Yeah, it was a difficult time."

"So you just decided to stay in Kansas City?"

"I had a good job and I liked it so much better than small town Oklahoma. Besides, there was no way I could go back to Spiro."

"Did you ever consider it?"

"Oh yes, many times."

"So what held you back? Was it just the small town?"

"There was no way I could ask Jettie to let me come back. I didn't have the nerve."

"The fact that you had a child together wasn't enough reason?"

"No, that was a very good reason. But Trevor, I didn't love Jettie enough to go back to him."

I didn't know how to feel about this new knowledge. It did shed a lot of light on some unanswered questions, but there still was Jettie, the man I've come to learn so much about, who was loved by so many, but not enough by the one he wanted it from most.

So when are you planning to come home?" she asked.

"I don't know."

"What do you mean you don't know? What about your degree? What about your job? I'm sure they'll let you come back if you want."

"Maybe I don't want to go back there."

"Then where will you go?"

"I still have more to do here."

"Like what?"

"That's my business, Mom."

"Your business? Trevor, I'm your mother."

"Yeah, and Jettie was my father. You had me for twenty-two years. Now it's his turn."

For a moment there was complete silence, then I could hear her weep.

"Mom? What's wrong?"

"Trevor, you're all I have in this world."

"Don't look at it that way."

"There's no other way to look at it."

"What are you so afraid of?"

"Never seeing you again."

"Well that's not possible. You just have to realize that I'm a grown man now and that I have to find my place in this world. And spending time here has helped me realize who I really am."

She sniffled.

"Well," she said, "you've obviously made up your mind."

I don't think there was anything I could say or do to help relieve her of her fear. Nevertheless, I was not about to sacrifice the opportunity to fill the empty hole that had formed inside of me; because not until then would I have the capability to help Mom fill hers.

THIRTY

wenty-four teenage boys dressed in faded Wranglers, T-shirts, straw cowboy hats and dusty boots stood in a half-circle around Boyd and squinted from the bright sunlight as he showed them a technique of adding rosin to rigging handles, and how to help another cowboy secure his glove with leather straps.

"For the most part it's rider against bull," he said. "But in the chute we help each other out."

The boys paired off and took turns practicing the teamwork of glove tying and Boyd walked around watching and instructing. After that activity we worked a bull into a small square pen and Boyd had the boys gather around.

"Does anybody know who this bull is?" he asked the group.

One boy raised his hand. He was short and stocky and dark-complected.

"What's your name?" Boyd asked.

"Carlos."

"Okay, Carlos, what do you know about this bull?"

"His name is Big Banana."

"Very good. And how did you know that?"

"My cousin rode him once in Oklahoma City."

"And what did you learn about Big Banana when your cousin rode him?"

"He bucks hard and likes to sunfish, but doesn't spin much."

"That's excellent. You're a very observant cowboy."

Carlos gleamed with pride.

"Gentlemen, Carlos has just taught us one of the first things you need to know about being a bull rider. It's not all about who's got the most guts and how well you can impress the ladies. It's a sport and a profession. And to be a professional you got to know who your adversaries are. Sure, you're competing against other riders for the highest score, but your concentration needs to be on the bull. You have to know how he rides. Learn his history and try not to be intimidated by his statistics no matter how successful he is."

I stood next to Jeremiah, who leaned against the fence behind Boyd and the group of youngsters.

"Did I hear him right?" I asked.

"Hard to believe, ain't it?"

"Doesn't seem like the same Boyd."

"I doubt he shares the lesson he had the other night."

"He's actually doing a great job with these kids."

"Yeah, and I don't think he even realizes it."

"Has he ever done this before?"

"Not that I know of."

"Look at those kid's faces. They're taken by him."

"Give it time, and maybe he'll be taken by them, too."

Later on in the afternoon a bus full of grade school age kids pulled into the arena parking lot. Jeremiah said they were part of a summer rodeo camp that was put on by a local community college. As part of the activities, they learned the fundamentals of riding by hopping on the backs of sheep and trying to stay on as they ran across the arena. Mutton bustin', they called it. The first one to reach the other side of the arena without falling off wins a special belt buckle. I also learned that this was an official event in Little Britches Rodeo.

The kids had a ball, and they especially liked all the attention they received by the teenage boys. But nothing compared to the attention they received from Boyd, and being a professional rodeo man, they swarmed around him asking a plethora of questions and occasionally for autographs. He obliged several of them, and later said that they should all get Carlos' autograph, that someday he was going to be a very famous rodeo champion. The kids did like he said and swarmed around Carlos as well.

He laughed as he watched them in their excitement, and when he looked our way he lost his smile—not in a way that seemed angry or contemptuous, but possibly of embarrassment, that maybe he had caught himself having a good time, or just doing something good, period.

After the little britches boarded back onto the bus and we all bid them a kind farewell, the young cowboys gathered around for their next lesson, which involved respect for animals and proper use of equipment. Since Jeremiah was a stock contractor with a personal interest in the health of the livestock, this was his platform. Not only did he inform them of the amount of care that goes into raising and providing stock for rodeos, but also the consequences for mishandling or damaging the animals. He also explained to them how to be a good sport if they ever experienced an animal with an ailment.

"If you see a horse or a bull limping, then it's your responsibility to report it. The last thing you want to do is think you have some sort of edge over that animal just because he's hurt. You're likely to be disqualified and possibly fined if the judges find out about it. Besides that, you're likely to get an ass kickin' from me!"

The boys chuckled.

"And that doesn't just apply to bucking stock. Same goes for any animal in any event. Respect the stock and the sport and in turn it will respect you."

When it came time to talk about equipment, such as spurs, chaps, and vests, Jeremiah had his talk about safety then Boyd took over.

Jeremiah decided it was time for a break and invited me to walk across the street with him to a dairy freeze. We walked up to a small window and gave our order to a young girl with braces who had slid open a small window and talked to us through a screen. Jeremiah ordered a strawberry shake and I a Butterfinger malt. A few minutes later the girl brought us our order, both in large paper cups. Jeremiah's heaped with pink ice cream and chunks of strawberries, and mine with vanilla ice cream and chunks of Butterfinger candy bar. Both had a long red plastic spoon stuck in the top. We sat in the shade on a white picnic table by the dairy freeze and enjoyed our cool treat along with a little conversation.

"My mom called the other night," I said, after swallowing a mouthful of cold ice cream.

"How's Bonnie?"

"Scared. And wondering when I'm coming home."

"Did you tell her about riding the bull?"

"Shit, no. And I'm not going to, either."

He nodded and inserted a spoonful of strawberry ice cream into his mouth.

"You don't think I should, do you?"

"That's your business and none of mine."

"I'm afraid if she knew, she'd be down here trying to stop me. And I don't want that."

"Do you think she could stop you?"

I pondered this over another spoonful of malt. "No."

"Then why worry about it. Maybe you should invite her down."

"No, I think that would ruin my concentration."

"Well, then maybe it's best."

"Yeah, maybe."

We each reached the bottoms of our cups and scraped the remaining contents out with our spoons.

"How soon can I ride again?"

"How's the wrist feel?"

I rotated it and flexed my fingers out in front of me. "Feels pretty good."

Jeremiah grabbed it and looked at it. "Looks better. Tomorrow I'll take another bull down to the arena and we'll go again."

"What do you mean, another bull? I haven't mastered Big Banana yet."

"You don't need to master that bull. You need to get on a spinner."

"I do?"

"Cyclone was an occasional spinner. You said you wanted to ride a bull like Cyclone."

I did want to ride a bull like Cyclone, but not as bad as I wanted to ride the *real* Cyclone. But I had also thought a lot about my last request to ride him, and that maybe I was being selfish to their feelings.

"You're right," I said. "But I want to apologize for that."

"For what?"

"I didn't know Jettie like you did. And when I said I wanted to ride Cyclone, I wasn't being sensitive to yours or anybody else's feelings."

Jeremiah smiled and patted me on the shoulder. "Don't worry about it. I know you didn't intend it that way."

Later that evening, parents, friends and other family members filled the bleachers to watch their teen wannabes demonstrate what they had learned. I went behind the scenes and watched Jeremiah and Boyd continue to coach the boys, and was learning a lot myself about what to do and what to expect in my own ride. Though each day that went by I became more and more familiar with the procedure of riding a bull, I was no less fearful about the dangers that lie ahead. I watched these young boys, who were eager to be just like Boyd someday. To travel the circuit all season long. Brave the circumstances and challenge the odds to one day compete at the National Finals. And my goal was quite the opposite. All I wanted was one ride and for a much different purpose.

Though at first I had worried a lot about Boyd and what he might do to hinder my chances for a successful ride, I was no more relieved, even though I felt as though my issue with him was behind me. The real challenge was still out there and not completely defined. So no different than yesterday, or the day I arrived in Spiro, my mind was still bogged down with uncertainty. And now, as I watched the young boys, wide-eyed and full of adrenaline, climb on the back of snorting, angry bulls, I was certain they were some of the most courageous young men in the world.

THIRTY-ONE

I worked out as early as possible to avoid the heat of the day. Wearing my workout shorts, tank top and running shoes I ran the narrow blacktop streets of Spiro, waving at the early risers who had become somewhat used to seeing me every now and then. Even now the old gentlemen with the flyswatter and thick glasses felt comfortable enough to offer a kind good morning. The town wasn't as sleepy as I thought, they just took their time getting used to strangers.

Every so often I would stop running and walk a short distance to slow my heart rate, then pick up pace again to give myself a thorough cardiovascular workout. Now at a steady jog, I had reached the far east side of town and the rodeo arena came into view. I stopped at the arena, looked at my watch then placed my fingertips on my neck and checked my heart rate. It had increased twelve beats in fifteen seconds since I left the house. Not bad for a slow run, I thought.

I decided to walk for a few minutes and walked around the arena. I had never really looked so closely at the place before, or noticed how simple everything seemed compared to the other arenas I had been to this summer. The white paint on the chutes and fence all around was peeling and showing rust. The bleacher sections were small with weathered wooden bench seats rather than aluminum or even plastic bleacher type seats they had in Mesquite. And the chutes and fences in the other arenas looked new with colorful graphic signs advertising beer, boots, jeans or chewing tobacco. In contrast the Spiro arena was a simple place, where the glitter and glamour didn't matter, only the feel of the hot sun and the smell of sweaty bull flesh, along with the ruggedness to take them both on.

I came back to the arena later that day and Jeremiah had already arrived. So had the two young cowboys who now had been formally introduced as Jason and Tate. Also in the arena was an older man riding a tractor and pulling a device that Jeremiah called a harrow. He said that the man worked for the city and had been loosening up the dirt at the baseball and softball diamonds across the road and he asked if he'd come and do the same at the arena. "Makes the dirt a little softer for the landing," he said.

I put on all my gear; the chaps and spurs and applied rosin to the rigging handle like I had learned from Boyd. Tate helped me tie on my glove and then I applied rosin to it as well.

Jeremiah had already unloaded the bull into the chute. He was a red Brangus with thick stubby horns and a black nose. He stood perfectly still inside the narrow chute and not at all fidgety. I knew nothing about this bull and the only source I had was Jeremiah.

"His name is Bloody Mary," he said.

"A bull named Mary? That hardly fits."

"Yeah, but the bloody part fits him real well."

"Oh."

Jeremiah went on to tell me that, like Cyclone, this bull was an occasional spinner. That likely, before the gate flew completely open, he would already have done half a turn. And he always goes left. After that, nobody knows what he's gonna do next."

"How many successful rides?"

"Zero."

"No one even close?"

"Five seconds is the best so far."

I had most of it down. I knew the bull's history but not so confident in how he would ride. So as I looked at him I rode him in my mind, thinking of how a quick spin left would feel, and then how to deal with the unexpected.

A truck pulled up behind the arena and the engine stopped. It was a bright blue short bed Chevy, raised high on wide all-terrain tires. I had only seen one truck like it, and it belonged to Boyd.

He stepped down and came walking toward us. He wore a black T-shirt and dark Oakley sunglasses under his straw hat and he removed them before he reached the fence.

"Howdy," he said.

I nodded.

"Howdy," Jeremiah said.

Boyd bent over and crawled through the fence and approached the chute. He put a stem of the sunglasses between his teeth and looked the bull over.

"Bloody Mary?"

"The one and only," Jeremiah said.

"Never been rode."

"Never."

He looked at me.

"You ready?"

"I have a good idea how he'll come out of the chute, but that's about it."

"Well, that's a good start. Just hunker down and cowboy up."

Boyd put his sunglasses back on, crawled back through the fence and went to the bleachers. He sat down and leaned back on his elbows.

Jeremiah and I climbed above the chute and attached the rigging and flank strap. The bull was no longer still and docile. He jerked at every sudden tug we made on the gear. Once everything was secure Jason and Tate took their places in the arena. Jeremiah sat atop the fence next to me as I lowered myself onto Bloody Mary. Its reaction to my presence was not much different than when they attached the gear. But after each passing second it seemed to grow used to me.

Before Jeremiah helped me with the rigging he coached me about spurring.

"Now you know that the rowels of those spurs are dull and it's likely the bull can't even feel them. Spurring is nothing more than a way to get more points. It's hard enough just to concentrate on the ride, let alone thinking about driving your heels into the flank of a bull."

"Is there a good time to spur?"

"You have to get the feel for that yourself. It comes with experience."

"Then I guess there's no chance for that."

"No, but you can do a good spur out."

"What?"

"That's spurring when the gate opens."

"Spur out."

"That's right."

He put the finishing touches on the rigging, securing it in the palm of my hand, then climbed over the gate and stood with the latch rope in his hands. I held the chute rail with my right hand and went over the ride once more in my mind, thinking now about the spur out, the quick spin left, and then wondering if it would keep spinning. I was sure I had it down all I could. Now it was time for the real thing.

I took a deep breath, in my nose, out my mouth, and then nodded at Jeremiah. As the gate flew open I worked my heals back and Bloody Mary spun left just like they had said. I handled the spin out of the chute just fine, but just as if someone had turned a throttle, the bull spun faster, and before I knew it I was on the ground. This time I landed on my hip and felt no rush of pain. Jeremiah had opened the gate and the bull already ran out of the arena. Jason and Tate came to me but I was quickly on my feet.

"Bull's quite a spinner, huh?" Jason said.

"I'll say."

Jeremiah came to me. "That was a good spur out."

"Yeah, but a lot of good it did me."

"Ah, you'll do much better next time."

I glanced up at Boyd in the bleachers. He sat with his arms crossed and staring.

"All right," I said. "Let's get it back in the chute."

THIRTY-TWO

Within the next hour I rode two more times, once going three seconds, the second going four. Each time I felt as though I was improving, but now my body felt fatigued and I needed a break.

After the last ride Boyd got up from the bleachers, went to his truck and drove away. I wanted to talk to him hoping I could get some pointers, but obvious to me he wasn't quite ready to be that friendly.

The rest of us sat on the ground under a shade tree outside the arena and talked about the rides. To help cool off I drank spring water from a squeeze bottle and Jeremiah refreshed himself with the typical beer and cigarette. Jason and Tate each drank a plastic bottle of Mountain Dew, and when they were done they each retrieved a can of Copenhagen from their back pockets, pinched a small dip and put it inside their bottom lip, then used the empty Mountain Dew bottles as a spittoon. Jeremiah even got out his bottle of corn whiskey and passed it around. I declined but Jason and Tate were quick to accept. I could tell by the way they grinned at each other and tipped the bottle that it was their first time. And the results were about as dramatic as I remembered, laughs from Jeremiah included, but I didn't have a dip of chew to hack out with it. In one fashion or another, I guess all young men of this life have to lose their moonshine virginity sometime.

Jeremiah said I was doing great and that what I had to do now was find that grove. I wasn't sure I knew what he meant, but hoped that it would eventually come to me. What I had learned was that the bull seemed tireless and was capable of offering whatever challenge I desired. Though four seconds on a bull like Bloody Mary was not that great of an accomplishment for most riders, to me it was major. And even though it happened so quickly, to think of staying on twice as long made seconds seem like hours. I suddenly wondered if I'd be satisfied if success happened today. Satisfied to the point where I could put my entire past to rest, and allow the legend of Jettie Hodge to carry on without flaw.

We all turned our heads to look at a vehicle that turned into the arena parking lot. It was an older green Ford station wagon, and when it came to a stop nearby I recognized Buddy Wells in the driver's seat. Not far behind him a pickup pulling a trailer came in as well. It was a new silver extended cab Chevy pickup that pulled a matching silver trailer. The truck had Texas license plates and I didn't recognize the heavyset man that drove it.

Buddy got out of his car, smiled and waved at us, then opened the back door of his station wagon and pulled out some clothing on wire hangers. He also grabbed a blue plastic sack, closed the door with his foot then came walking toward us.

The heavyset man in the pickup stepped out as well. He wore a red farm cap, short sleeved western shirt, dark blue jeans and dusty boots. He nodded and smiled at Jeremiah.

"About time y'all got here," Jeremiah said, standing to shake the heavyset man's hand. "Trevor's already rode twice."

Their presence was obviously planned and for a reason that Jeremiah had failed to tell me about. Buddy smiled at me and suddenly I recognized that the clothing he carried on the hangers was clown apparel. He asked me about my rides and I told him about them in the briefest manner possible, then made way for my own question.

"So what are you doing here?"

He pointed down at Jason and Tate. "Oh, Jeremiah thought it best to relieve these youngsters of their duties and bring a real clown into the arena."

I looked at the clothes again and studied his face for sincerity. "No shit?"

"Hey, when it comes to clown work this boy doesn't clown around."

I'm sure my smile was a timid one as he laughed and slapped me on the arm and then shook my hand. I couldn't think of a better way to ride and feel the presence of camaraderie the way my father had than with Buddy in the arena with me. Nothing could have added more to my confidence, and I suddenly felt the bond of friendship he and Jettie once had.

Buddy turned his head to the heavyset man. "Trevor, I'd like you to meet Paul Baldwin from Midland, Texas."

We shook hands and Paul offered condolences and compliments about Jettie, and at the same time I tried to figure out why all the sudden his presence had a stroke of familiarity.

Jeremiah came to my aid. "Trevor, old Baldy here is a stock contractor and come Thursday night he's going to supply the bull that you drew for your ride."

First of all, Thursday night was two nights away and I knew nothing about a scheduled rodeo. But then it came to me. Cyclone, the infamous bull, was sold to a contractor in Midland, Texas. I looked toward his trailer, and through the corrugated rails saw the silhouette of a bull.

"You mean to tell me—"

"That's right," Jeremiah said. "For Thursday night's rodeo, you drew Cyclone."

"I don't know what to say."

"You don't have to say nothing," Buddy said. "You just have to get back on Bloody Mary and get to practicing."

"Bloody Mary?"

"That's right," Jeremiah said. "In the meantime, Cyclone will be right here at the arena for you to study"

"I see. So how did you arrange for me to be in a rodeo?"

"Well, this is a special kind of rodeo. One event, one bull, one rider. Right here in this arena."

"You've arranged all that just for me?"

"Why the hell not?"

Realizing they were serious, I walked down to the trailer to get my first look at the bull that in part had changed so many people's lives. I peeked through the rails and tried not to rile him. He was mostly black with a white face and thick ivory horns cut flat on the ends. He also had a large hump, which indicated the Brahma portion of his breeding. He acknowledged my presence by lowering his head and blowing through his nostrils. Dust and dried manure swirled from the floor of the trailer under his nose. Like Jeremiah had said, he looked no more dangerous than any other bull, but as fate would have it, this bull had an unchangeable mark. And come Thursday night, the opportunity would come for us both to challenge that history.

*   *   *

Buddy changed into his clown gear and he agreed to allow one of the boys to help him. Neither of them volunteered so he finally asked Tate to assist and he kindly accepted the task. And Buddy wouldn't allow him to be out of uniform, either. He gave him a straw cowboy hat painted florescent green along with a pair of bibbed overalls that looked three times his size and cut off at the knees. They sat down on the bleachers and Buddy painted his face white and red around the mouth. He did the same to himself by looking into a small portable mirror that he hung on one of the fence rails. The rest of the team helped me in the chute. Paul chose to be the gate man while Jeremiah and Jason helped me gear up. I rosined my glove and rigging handle again while Jeremiah went over the basics.

"Now you've been on this bull three times. You know what it does and how it feels."

I nodded.

He patted me on the shoulder. "Giver hell, cowboy!"

When the gate opened it was déjà vu. The bull spun left and kept spinning, only this time I felt more secure, and each time the bull bucked and shifted my balance was maintained. I could hear them yelling and cheering, and suddenly I heard the sound of a horn and jumped off. I landed on my hands and knees but quick back to my feet. Either the bull sensed its defeat or it was simply tired of me being on its back because it came for me. I ran quickly but it seemed to know the perfect angle to cut me off. But before it could get too close Buddy was there to deter it, and with the help of his protégé clown I was freed from the bull's wrath.

The bull found the opened gate and Paul closed it behind. Then they all came to me, Jeremiah and Buddy both offering congratulatory embraces while Jason and Tate offered high fives and Paul a firm handshake.

"You did it!" Jeremiah said. "You're now a full blown, pain in the ass cowboy!"

They continued to compliment me on how well I did, even though I'm not sure how I did it. As far as I knew, anyone could be an accountant. All it required was four years of college and the ability to live alone inside a cubicle forty hours a week. In bull riding one could learn the fundamentals in less than a week, but it required a certain physique as well as a ton of courage. So for me it was a remarkable triumph, so much that it made me fear the evening ahead. I'd had four chances at eight seconds with Bloody Mary, with only the pressure to learn and make it one step closer to my goal. But now Cyclone was the goal, and there would only be one chance to make it. And the pressure was not so much about making the time itself, but making the time for someone else. To display that kind of honor for a man I've come to know was the greatest pressure of all.

THIRTY-THREE

T he thick T-bone steaks sizzled on the grill next to two large potatoes wrapped in aluminum foil. With a small yellow brush I basted the steaks with barbeque sauce then laid the brush on a plate next to the grill. Flies buzzed around like vultures and landed on the brush once abandoned. No matter how vigorously I shooed them away they were persistent in their return.

The evening was still fairly hot and the heat from the grill made the backyard atmosphere that much hotter. And Buddy had mixed us each a hot toddy in thick plastic mugs and, save the heat and sweat on our foreheads, we were well into a feeling good stage.

We sat in lawn chairs and I watched over the meat while Buddy told me a few old rodeo tales as well as stories of past loves.

"I've had a lot of girlfriends, but only one could claim to have ever owned my heart, and the only girlfriend that I didn't meet at a rodeo."

"Ironic, huh?"

"Yeah. Her name was Valerie. I called her Val. She was a teacher at this elementary school where me and this other rodeo clown were invited to show off to the kids. The moment I laid eyes on her I knew I had to get to know her. She looked just like Gunilla Hutton on Hee Haw. You know who I'm talking about?"

"Can't say that I do."

"She was a damn looker, let me tell ya. Long, thick blonde hair, eyes bluer than the sky, and boy was she curvy."

"The outside sounds pretty good. But was that all you loved about her?"

"Oh no, she was a sweetheart. Treated me like a king."

"So what happened?"

"I asked her to marry me."

"That was a problem?"

"For her it was. She said that she couldn't and I never saw her again."

"And that was the love of your life?"

"Yessir, it was. And I cried all night over that woman."

"Really? Here I figured cowboys were too tough to cry."

"No sir, in fact a cowboy's heart is probably softer than any other man's. It's the skin that's tough."

"Soft heart, tough skin, hard head. Right?"

This made him chuckle a bit. "You've got it, pardner."

By the time the steaks and potatoes were ready, he had mixed us another toddy. Not much was said while we ate. Maybe an occasional compliment to the steak, or to the chef, but other than that it was the sound of cutting and chewing.

After the meal it was time for another toddy and we sat back in the lawn chairs, scratched our bellies and chewed on toothpicks.

"So what about you?" he asked. "You found the love of your life yet?"

I shrugged. "Couldn't tell ya."

"Ah, if you had you'd know it."

"I had a girlfriend back in KC. Amber. But she was more of a friend than anything else."

"Yeah, I had them, too. But not near the same thing."

"There used to be this Italian girl that lived up the street from me. She was twelve and I was fourteen. I'd ride my bike by her house as often as I could, hoping to see her. I guess you'd call it a crush. I thought about her a lot. Went to sleep every night with her on my mind."

"That's the feeling I'm talking about. 'Can't get her out of your head' kind of feelings."

"I never felt that way again until I met Bella."

"Well let me tell ya something, pardner. Miss Bella is as fine a woman as they come. Been through a lot in her life so it might be kind of tough to get her to open up, but man what a woman you'd have if she did."

"You really think so?"

"Hell yes! Don't you?"

"I just don't think we're very compatible."

"What the hell do you mean by that?"

"We were raised totally different."

"Well let me tell ya something else, pardner. When it comes to love, everybody is compatible."

"How can you say that?"

"You don't love somebody for what you want. And if you really love them, then you'll let them enjoy being themselves."

"That makes sense, but it makes it hard to be together."

"I didn't say you have to be together."

"Then what good is loving someone if you can't be with them?"

"I guess it's just my theory, but I don't believe that you can chose who you love. I believe that love chooses you."

"I guess that explains you and Val, right?"

"That's right. I had no control over it. I saw her and I wanted her. And once I met her I loved her."

"But don't you think you could have done something to get her to be with you?"

"Sometimes that's the misery of love. Not everybody is as fortunate to be loved back. And it'll make a fella cry every time."

He went inside to the kitchen and mixed us another toddy while I pondered his love logic. Dusk was now upon us and occasionally a lightening bug would flash somewhere in a darkened area of the lawn. When he came back with our toddies I noticed that he stumbled, somewhat, and nearly upset the lawn chair as he sat down. But I didn't even realize how drunk I was getting until I rose from my chair to go to the bathroom. So the feeling good stage was behind us, and the drunken stage had arrived.

When I returned I sat slowly into the lawn chair and peered out into the darkness. Through the trees I could now see the stars, and at the bottom of the grill a few charcoals still glowed a fiery orange. The only light upon us now shined through the kitchen window. It was not much, but enough to highlight Buddy's profile and attract a swarm of moths, June bugs and hundreds of tinier flying insects.

"You know," I said, "I've never cried for a girl before."

"Never?"

"I wonder if I ever will."

"You're bound to sometime. I guess it's the one way of knowing if you really love someone."

"How so?"

"Well, you either cry because you're afraid you're gonna lose them, or you cry because you have."

"You think Jettie ever cried?"

"Jettie was a tough old bird, but I did see him cry once."

"You did?"

"In fact it was a night just like tonight. Right here at this house."

"What was he crying about?"

"Couldn't tell you. We had just got back from a rodeo up in Springdale, Arkansas. We decided to mix a couple toddies and before we knew it we was damn near walking on our knees."

"And he just started crying?"

"No, he said he had to go take a leak and he got to taking a long time about it so I went to see if he was all right. I went to the bathroom and the door was open and he wasn't in there. I heard sniffling and that's when I looked through the bedroom door. He was sitting on the floor next to the bed, elbows on his knees looking at something and crying."

"What was he looking at?"

"Don't know. I asked him if he was all right and that startled him. He wiped his eyes and whatever he was looking at he stuffed between the bed mattresses and walked out of the room. He went plumb out the back door and I never saw him again until morning."

"And you never asked him what it was about?"

"I figured if he wanted me to know he'd have told me."

"How long ago was this?"

"Hell, I don't know. Fifteen, maybe twenty years ago."

I wasn't sure why I lingered on this topic, but for some reason the thought of seeing a man like Jettie—who everybody loved for his heroic and manly distinction—cry, seemed very much out of character. But then again he was a man, like any other man, who had his private side and dealt with misery in his own way.

Another hour and two toddies later Buddy and I decided to sing. He tried to teach me a few cowboy songs, like *Tumbling Tumbleweeds* by Sons of the Pioneers, *Mamas, Don't Let Your Babies Grow Up To Be Cowboys* by Willie Nelson and Waylon Jennings, then a finale of *Killin' Time* by Clint Black. I knew that one so we sang it together.

Then we resorted to telling silly jokes and laughing until our stomachs hurt.

"You know what priests and Christmas trees have in common?" Buddy asked.

I shook my head, already laughing.

"They both have balls but they're just for decoration!"

I fell out of my chair laughing and so did Buddy. We looked up at each other and we laughed so hard we cried. We rolled around on the ground like a couple of mad hyenas, and eventually wore ourselves to the point we couldn't take anymore. We both sat on our knees, trying not to look at each other but still laughed when we did. Then Buddy tipped his mug and sucked down the last of his toddy.

"I'm ready for another one," he said in a drunken slur. "But I don't think I can stand up.

We both laughed again and tried to help each other up. Arm-in-arm we walked into the kitchen, laughing and stumbling over each other's feet and singing again the chorus to *Killin' Time*.

"You make the toddies," he said. "I've got to take a piss."

"Are you sure you can walk?"

"If I can't then I'll crawl."

He laughed all the way through the kitchen, stumbling and falling against the walls.

I made us both another drink but Buddy never returned to the kitchen. I worked my way to the bathroom and found him passed out on the floor. It was all I could do to pick him up and carry him to the davenport, so that's where I left him for the night.

I worked my way back to the bathroom to make my own attempt at urinating. I held one hand against the wall for support, and as I thought about the evening I laughed and found myself urinating on the floor. But because of my good cheer I thought nothing of it, finished the job and went on my way.

I started to go back to the kitchen to get my toddy when I stopped at the bedroom door and looked inside the room. I reached around the wall and flicked on the light switch and looked down at the bed. After staring at the bed for a moment, I walked toward it, dropped slowly to my knees and put one hand on top of the bed while the other felt between the mattresses. I slid my hand from left to right until finally I felt a slick piece of paper, pulled it out and saw that it was an older color photograph, rectangular with rounded corners, like from a 110 camera.

I slid down to where I sat on the floor and leaned my back against the bed. I rested my elbows on my knees and looked at the photo closely, at the young man in western apparel, about my size maybe thinner, with hair over his ears and a cowboy hat pushed back on his head. He smiled proudly, and in his arms he held a baby—a hand underneath its bottom as if to show it off. It was bald headed with rounded eyes and fat cheeks, and it smiled slightly with a line of slobber hanging from its mouth. And next to the man and the baby was a woman. I recognized her immediately. Her smile seemed sincere, and she was young and beautiful.

Reddish orange numbers were imprinted on the lower left-hand corner of the photo. They read "07 77".

As I held the photo with one hand and ran the fingers of my other hand through my hair, I studied the faces in the photo—particularly Jettie's face, as he revealed himself in a manner that no man could have taken away.

I turned the photo over, took a heavy breath and looked down between my knees. The mixture of whiskey and hot water, along with a wealth of sudden emotion, made me feel as though my blood was expanding in my veins. But rather than rupturing internally it seemed to convert itself to air and discharge through my lungs, and once the largest part of it was gone, all my energy was exhausted, then all I could do was cover my eyes and weep.

THIRTY-FOUR

T he next day I woke with a splitting headache. I rose
from the bed and the sun knifed through the window
and shined on my face. I rolled away and squinted at the
clock on the nightstand. It was almost one-thirty.

I was still in my clothes and smelled badly of stale charcoal
smoke and whiskey. I moved slowly to the living room and saw
that Buddy was gone. I guess he was a lot more used to whiskey
hangovers than I was.

I stood under the hot shower streams longer than usual, and
after the shower I put on a pair of old Levi jeans, T-shirt, work
boots and a red and black cap that advertised Justin boots. For
breakfast I fried some bacon and scrambled eggs and, rather than
my usual orange juice, I drank a can of Pepsi and took three
aspirin. After that I chewed and swallowed three desperately
needed antacid tablets.

Though it was pretty late in the day and I didn't feel much up
to anything, I decided to drive out to the ranch and see what
Jeremiah and Boyd were up to. But before I had a chance to shut
and lock the front door, Bella appeared in front of it.

"Hi," I said.

"Hi."

I invited her in. She was dressed in denim shorts, a red spaghetti strapped top and white sandals. A black purse hung over her shoulder, keys dangled in her hand, and she carried a white box under her arm. The box was made of thin cardboard, like a gift box from a department store only deeper, about the same dimensions as a boot box.

"Surprised you're still here," she said.

"Just got up."

"Just now?"

"Buddy and I got a little drunk last night."

She smirked. "Hung over?"

"Severely."

"Let me guess, hot toddies?"

"Now what made you say that?"

"Oh, just a hunch. So where were you headed?"

"I thought I'd go out to the ranch, see what the boys are up to."

"So how's Boyd's social rehab going?"

"He worked great with the youngsters. Might make a man out of him yet."

She laughed and set the box on the davenport.

"What's that?" I asked.

"Oh, just a little something I want you to have."

"You bought me a present?"

"No, it's something that used to belong to Jettie and I want you to have it for tomorrow night."

"So you know about my little rodeo?"

"Everybody knows."

"Everybody?"

"The whole town. Expect a full house."

"How'd they know? This isn't an official event."

"Trevor, this is Spiro, Oklahoma. Population 2,146. All you have to do is tell the lady down at the convenience store, or tell Barney down at the café, and like a swift wind the word gets around."

"I don't know what to say. It's more than I expected."

"Hey, you wanted to ride in a rodeo, didn't you?"

"Well, yeah, but—"

"Then don't complain, you got you're wish."

"Are you going to be there?"

She paused and looked out the door and into the street. "I'm thinking about it."

"Well, it would mean a lot if you were there."

She nodded then looked down at the box. "Aren't you going to open it?"

"Oh, yeah."

I sat down on the davenport and pulled off the top section of the box. I flipped back the tissue paper to reveal a black leather garment.

I looked up at her. "What is this?"

"Pull them out and look at them."

I did as she said then stood and let them unfold in front of me. They were a pair of chaps, glossy black with white leather fringe all down the sides, and royal blue letters outlined in white. They spelled "JETTIE" on one leg and "HODGE" on the other.

"These are amazing," I said.

"They were a gift to Jettie the year he quit riding. He would have worn them, but he retired before he had the chance."

"Who gave them to him?"

"I did."

"You?"

"Yeah, I had them custom made. And since they weren't going to get used I kept them at my place. They'd have just gathered dust here."

"These are very special. Why are you giving them to me?"

"I bought them for a bull rider. I figured you'd like to wear them tomorrow night."

"I will."

"Great. Well I guess I'll get going."

She turned to go and I set the chaps back down in the box. "Wait."

She turned back to me and I stared at her like a lost child.

She laughed. "Were you going to say something?"

"I really don't know what to say. I just want to thank you, I guess."

"For the present? Hey, it's no big deal."

"No, not just the present. For everything."

"Everything?"

"Yeah. It's been a crazy summer for me, and you've added so much life to it."

"Are you sure about that?"

"I'm very sure."

She smiled slightly but it quickly vanished. "I have to go."

"All right."

"Good luck tomorrow."

"Thanks."

Just like every other time I watched her walk away, there was a certain part of me that ached and longed to go after her. But there was also a part of me that wallowed in fear, and from that I lacked confidence. So for those reasons alone, I refrained, knowing that she was someone I couldn't bear to let down.

*   *   *

I drove out to the ranch and, rather than working, I found Boyd and Jeremiah sitting in the horse barn drinking beer. Jezebel lay sleeping on her belly on the concrete with her chin between her front legs. She opened her eyes and looked at me then closed them again. Boyd sat on the floor, his back against the barn wall and legs crossed and stretched out in front of him. Jeremiah sat on a bale of hay and greeted me enthusiastically then offered me a beer.

"No thanks," I said

"Oh bullshit! Why not?"

"A little hung over, that's why."

"Keep on drinking. That's my motto."

He and Boyd laughed.

"So what's on the agenda today?" I asked.

He held up his beer bottle. "What does it look like?"

I sat down on an upside-down bucket.

"No," Jeremiah said, "not much to do around here. Just getting ready for your wing ding tomorrow night." He nudged Jezebel with the toe of his boot. "Ain't that right Jezzie?"

She lifted her head, perked her ears and looked back at him. Seemingly annoyed, she laid her head back down and closed her eyes.

A voice from outside the barn called Jeremiah's name. It was Jodie. She said he had a telephone call.

"Ah, hell!" he said. "Doesn't everybody know I took the afternoon off?"

He left the barn and Jezebel followed him out, leaving Boyd and I in an awkward circumstance. There was a short period of silence then Boyd was the first to speak.

"So you and Buddy get pretty wasted last night?"

"I'd say. Been a long time since I've been that drunk."

"Yeah, the last big drunk I remember was down in Fort Worth."

His face remained fairly firm with a light smirk. I had no idea where he was going, but nonetheless, he made me nervous.

He peeled a piece of label off his beer bottle and threw it on the concrete floor. "But I deserved every damned bit of it."

I didn't know what to say, but I was glad to hear him confess.

"Now I don't want to kiss or hug or anything," he said. "And you'll never hear me say it again."

"Say what?"

"That I'm sorry about what happened to Jettie. It was a stupid prank and I'll never do anything like it again."

I knew he was sincere but didn't really know how to respond, so I simply nodded and allowed his apology to penetrate the air.

"So you ready for tomorrow night?" he asked.

"Hell, I don't know. Ready as I'll ever be, I guess."

"You'll make a fine bull rider. Lots of talent—just like your pa."

"You really think so?"

"I ain't lying, dude. You have the sand and the smarts. You'll do alright."

I didn't quite know how to respond to such a compliment. I never intended to let on that I wanted to be a pro bull rider. It was just something I wanted to learn. Something I had to do for me. But rather than negate the only kindness I'd ever received from Boyd, I decided to simply accept the compliment and go on to something else.

"Looks like you'll make the finals this year," I said.

"Still a lot of season left. But this is the best year I've ever had."

"You know, Jeremiah says a lot of good things about your talents."

"Yeah, all accept my attitude, right?"

"Never said anything about that."

He threw another piece of label onto the floor. "Yeah, well I know it's true."

"If you really feel that way, then you're the only one who can change it."

"Did you know my daddy is in prison?"

"No, I didn't."

"He got caught stealing horses. Not one time, but five. He'd watch the rodeos for lame stock, steal them, then take them down to the dog food factory in Fort Worth."

"They bought stolen horses from him?"

"They didn't care. They gave so much per pound and before long the evidence was gone."

"What a racket."

"Yeah, he just couldn't quit the habit."

"How long is he in for?"

"Oh, he'll be out in a couple years. Been in for five, since I was in high school."

"If it's any consolation, I understand what it's like to not have a father around."

"The only father figure I had was my uncle. The lawman who helped my pa get away with stealing the horses."

"Well, maybe you should hang around Jeremiah more. Drinks a lot, but other than that he's a pretty good man."

"Yeah, I like Jeremiah."

"And he knows rodeo. A guy like that might come in handy."

Boyd just smiled and nodded.

"So what are you gonna do after your big ride?" he asked.

"I'm not sure. I figure after the ride I'll know."

He tipped his beer bottle high and drank the last of its contents. "Well," he said, then licked his lips. "If you want to ride the circuit, you're welcome to ride along with me."

I laughed under my breath. "I'll consider that."

He tossed his beer bottle into a nearby trash container and it crashed among other bottles.

"I reckon Jeremiah will be back in a minute," he said. "I better get back to work."

"Doing what?"

"The cooler is behind you, *amigo*. Hand me another beer."

THIRTY-FIVE

After a good night's sleep I rose a little before nine to prepare for my big day. First was my workout. Sit-ups and curls and I ran my typical course around town, getting more smiles and "good mornings" than usual from the townsfolk.

A little before noon I drove outside of town to the cemetery. The reddish brown dirt over Jettie's grave had settled somewhat, and grass was starting to grow. This was the first I'd seen the headstone, and the first I'd ever seen his real name, Jedidiah "Jettie" Franklin Hodge. On top of the headstone was an engraving of a cowboy riding a bronc. I guess the engraver didn't know how to carve out a bull. And below his name were the traditional dates of birth and death, and at the base a silver vase holding wilted flowers. Inscribed above the base was a short epitaph.

He came out of the chute like a jet, and rode with the pride of twenty spirited cowboys.

I imagine to most people that probably said it all. But to me I knew that there was more in his heart and his mind than just staying on that bull.

I squatted and removed my hat. "I'm not sure whether or not you can hear me. The preacher at your funeral said that your spirit would always be shining down upon us from heaven. Well, if that's true then I hope your spirit is listening.

"Things may or may not have been different for you and me if we'd have known each other. Amazing how a boy can grow up so oblivious to the idea of knowing or even having a father. Well, I sure did. But I'm grateful for this summer here in Oklahoma, because now I've learned the best part of you. You were a good man, Jettie Hodge."

I stood and put my hat back on then hung the golden tassel from my commencement cap around the flowers in the vase. Though it represented an educational accomplishment elsewhere, I figured there was no touching the higher order of learning I had received here this summer.

I turned to walk away, but quickly stopped.

"Oh, and one more thing. If there is any chance that you can be there tonight, there's a rodeo going on at the Spiro arena. Yeah, I know I won't be able to see you, but it would sure be nice to feel your presence."

* * *

I looked through all of Jettie's old clothing and accessories to pick out an outfit for the big event. I knew it didn't have to be anything fancy, but I wanted to look good for the crowd, in a way Jettie would have looked.

For boots I chose a pair of black ropers that appeared to be broke in well and very durable. They were a bit dusty so I wiped them off with a damp cloth then set them aside. I chose the best pair of Levi's I could find, which were not as faded as the others but still a lighter blue. And for a shirt I chose a red denim western shirt. It was slightly faded but very comfortable, but also it went excellent with the fancy chaps. When I laid the outfit on the bed and looked it over, I was impressed with the appeal.

For a hat I chose the best straw he had, which was a Stetson Bella said he'd only worn on special occasions. Well, to me this was a special occasion.

I chose a black belt with silver conchos all around, and after looking though the buckles there was only one that stood out among the rest. It was the Bud Light Cup buckle with the red, white and blue triangular logo in the center. It was handsome and went well with all the other apparel.

I set everything aside and heard a knock on the door then a voice. It was a female voice and I figured it was Bella visiting again. But when I walked into the living room it was not Bella that stood inside my door, but the last person on earth I would expect to see.

She crossed her arms and delivered a wry smile, looking no different than usual, her hair short and styled, wearing an olive colored sleeveless blouse, off-white slacks and matching heeled shoes. A taupe colored purse hung from a strap around her shoulder. And suddenly I smelled her perfume, which I'm sure was a brand I'd never heard of and an expensive gift from a past boyfriend.

"Mom—what are you doing here?"

She continued with her stale look and gazed around the room. "I haven't seen this place in years."

I looked around with her. "I guess it hasn't changed much."

She shook her head. "No, not really."

"So why this surprise visit?"

"Oh, I got a call from your grandmother, who heard from your grandfather, who heard from Jeremiah that you were riding a bull in a rodeo tonight."

"Jeremiah told Grandpa?"

"I guess he thought he'd like to come and watch."

"I guess so."

"So I called Jeremiah yesterday to find out what was going on, and he filled me in."

Now she stared scornfully at me.

"What's going on, Trevor?"

"You don't understand—"

"No, I don't. Please explain it to me."

"You haven't been here, Mom. You haven't seen things from my point of view."

"What have they done? Brainwashed you?"

"Come on, Mom. You know me better than that."

She laughed sarcastically. "Do I?" She let the purse strap fall down her arm then set the purse on the floor and walked around the living room looking at things. Her footsteps on the hardwood floor were the only sound in the room. "I thought I knew you before you quit your job."

"Things change, Mom. And I'm glad I did it."

She looked squarely at me now, her arms crossed again. "I can accept the fact that you needed to learn who your father was, but why this bull ride? Please explain the purpose of that?"

"No, Mom, first you need to explain some things to me."

"Like what?"

"I know there's a lot of broken marriages in this world. One moment they feel they can't live without each other and then all of the sudden they can't stand each other. And by that time a kid has come along and behold, we have a broken family. Why? Because of selfishness."

"There's probably a lot of truth to that."

"But how could anybody do that? How could *you*, my mother, go to the length of marrying a man, committing to him for life, give him a child, then take all of it away?"

"You don't know what it was like, Trevor."

"Maybe I do."

"How could you? All Jettie wanted was the goddamn rodeo. He didn't care about me. And he certainly didn't care about you."

"Oh really?" I went into the bedroom and retrieved the shoebox full of letters, which now also obtained the photograph I had found between the mattresses. I took the box out and handed it to her. I took off the lid and threw it on the floor and held the picture in front of her. My eyes were now glazed with tears. "Does this look like a man who didn't love his son? Does it look like a man who wasn't proud of his family?"

She took the photo gingerly and I could tell it was difficult for her to look at. A single tear ran down her cheek and after she looked at it for a short moment she closed her eyes.

"If you would have read those letters, Mom, and not returned them, you would have known just how much Jettie needed his family. You would have known that you could have come back and worked things out."

She took the box over to the davenport, sat down and started shuffling through the letters. After she had looked at all of them, she looked up at me. "I've never seen these before."

"What are you talking about?"

"It must have been Darrin. He must have returned them."

"Darrin?"

"He always got the mail before I did. And he hated Jettie."

"But you saw the one that Jeremiah brought to the graduation. Why didn't you say something then?"

"I guess I was so shocked to see him that I didn't pay that much attention to it. I just wanted him to leave."

"But in one of those letters he talks about coming up to see you and you calling the cops. What was that all about?"

"Yes, I remember that night. Jettie came to talk to me. He said that he wanted to see you and Darrin wouldn't let him. Jettie persisted so Darrin called the police."

"Well forget Darrin. What did you want?"

"I don't know, Trevor."

She buried her face in the palm of her hands and wept. I went over to the davenport and sat beside her, eventually putting my arm around her.

It was obvious that at one time her entire life had slipped away from her. Maybe it was prompted by selfishness, but at this point I honestly believed she was unaware of Jettie's feelings. She didn't know the reasons he never made it as a rodeo champion. She didn't know it was because of a huge empty hole in his heart. He had lost his wife and his child, the most important part of his life, gone and not likely to never return. So it was doubtful he had much motivation to be the best. Who would he have to share the victory with? Who could he pass that legacy on to? No one. All he could do was get out there and ride.

My only wish is that I could have been there for him, so he could have looked up in the stands before every ride and smiled and waved at his wife and little boy, and maybe that would have been all the encouragement he needed to make that ride and be the best there ever was. But all I had was this summer, and now today.

Mom leaned her head against my shoulder. "I'm so sorry, Trevor."

"Me, too."

She looked up at me with red, tear-filled eyes. Her mascara ran and her wet lashes stuck together. "Is there anything I can do?"

"Just give me the benefit of the doubt and don't question what I have to do tonight."

"What if you get seriously hurt? Worse yet, what if you get killed?"

"That won't happen."

"How can you be so sure?"

"I just know and you have to trust me on that."

"Can't you please tell me what it's all for?"

"For my satisfaction. One ride for all the years missed."

She wiped at her tears and sniffled. "You really think that will make a difference?"

"If I stay on that bull tonight then I can go on and live the rest of my life knowing I gave something back to my father. Just one ride, Mom. That's all I need."

THIRTY-SIX

W hen I arrived at the arena I was surprised to see it had received a dramatic facelift. Small plastic flags that advertised Coors beer were strung on a rope that crisscrossed above the arena from light pole to light pole and flapped in the evening breeze. The old man with the tractor and harrow drove circles inside the arena loosening, and in my case softening the dirt. The parking lot had completely filled with vehicles and people were now parking street side. Spectators walked across the parking lot toward the arena, some carried folded lawn chairs while others piled into the bleachers. The concession stand had opened and was already doing business, fans of the rodeo walking away with their hands loaded down with a mix of drinks, hot dogs, popcorn, or nachos with melted cheese and jalapenos. Speakers had been mounted on the poles and now played instrumental music, a tune that sounded like the beginning of the old *Dallas* TV show.

I went to the camper that Jeremiah had set up for Paul Baldwin and found both Paul and Jeremiah inside drinking a beer, along with Jason (who I thought was drinking Mountain Dew but noticed a bulge in his bottom lip and watched him spit into the bottle), Buddy and Tate dressed in clown apparel, and Denny Rose who looked as usual in a white dress western shirt with a bolo tie and gray felt cowboy hat.

"Hey, there's the man of the hour!" Jeremiah said.

They all greeted me with howdys and pats on the shoulder and handshakes.

"What is all this?" I asked. "Looks like a circus out there."

"Not far from it, wouldn't you say?" Buddy said.

"You wanted a rodeo," Jeremiah said, "so you got a rodeo."

"I don't know what to say."

"Don't say anything," Buddy said. "Just get out there and do your best."

"Jason and I will be in the chute with you, if that's okay," Jeremiah said.

Jason grinned with the dip in his lip.

"Perfect," I said.

Buddy slapped Tate on the knee. "Yeah and old Tate here says he kind of liked the clown biz so he's joining me in the arena."

"Damn," I said. "Add an announcer and rock and roll music to all this and it'd almost be official."

"Took care of that, too," Jeremiah said.

Denny rounded his eyes and grinned then raised his hand and waved. "What song would you like me to play, pardner?"

"You guys are great," I said, shaking his hand again.

"Hey, anything for Jettie's boy." Denny said.

"Well," I said, "let's all go out there one more time for Jettie."

"Amen," Buddy said.

*   *   *

Unlike the other rodeos I had been to, Denny announced from inside the arena on horseback. He rode a strawberry roan gelding and carried a cordless microphone. The crowd consisted of people of all ages. Jeremiah said he didn't ever remember seeing this many people in the Spiro arena before. I studied them as closely as possible, recognizing very few, only some of the townspeople I'd met during my morning runs. But I did recognize Barney from the restaurant and his waitress Tanya. There was the preacher from the funeral and many others I had seen there as well. Eileen from the sale barn café sat close to the chutes. She chewed gum and drank a cup of beer and winked when she caught my glance. Then I saw Grandpa and Grandma, sitting in lawn chairs on the other side of the arena fence. Grandpa, no doubt wore a jumpsuit, light blue denim with short bottoms and he wore white socks up to his knees and white shoes. They both smiled and waved.

"With this kind of turnout," I said, "maybe you should start having rodeos in Spiro."

"This is no ordinary rodeo," Jeremiah said. "It kind of has a fascination similar to a cockfight."

"A cockfight?"

"Yeah, people only know about it by word of mouth. And more than that, I'm sure there's a lot of betting going on."

"Betting?"

"Yeah, I'm sure there's a few greedy souls out there playing against the odds."

"You mean, betting that I will stay on rather than get my guts stomped out?"

"Exactly."

I looked for other faces I might recognize, and that's when I saw Bella pull up in her Mustang. She walked to the far end of the arena and rested her forearms on the top fence rail. She looked great, dressed in tight Lawman jeans and a sleeveless white shirt. She didn't wear a hat and her long black hair hung down over her shoulders and occasionally caught the light breeze. This whole arrangement was overwhelming, but for me I don't think it could have been entirely complete without her.

Denny's voice blared over the speakers. "Welcome, ladies and gentlemen, to tonight's special event!"

The crowd grew quiet and listened intently.

"Now you all know that this is not your ordinary rodeo. Tonight you're going to watch a young man pay a special tribute to his father, and hero of our community, Jettie Hodge."

Short applause.

"As most of you know, family, friends, and fans of rodeo lost Jettie almost two months ago in a tragic accident. Though he will be sorely missed, his legend lives on."

I watched the faces of the crowd. Most were solemn, a few men removed their hats, and some of the women wiped at their eyes. That's when I saw my mother, standing at the end of the bleachers, wearing the same clothes from earlier in the day, only now she wore a pair of brown designer sunglasses.

Denny continued. "Ladies and gentlemen, before I turn this mic over to Trevor, we're going to hear a few words from a very special man of this community. He's been around rodeo all his life, and to this day remains one of the most respected rodeo men in the country. Without further a due, I introduce former PRCA stock contractor of the year, and brother of Jettie Hodge, the one and only Jeremiah Hodge!"

The crowd applauded and cheered as Jeremiah trotted across the arena and grabbed the microphone. I was anxious to hear what he had to say, but also terrified to suddenly learn that I was also expected to say a few words to the crowd.

"Good evening, everyone," Jeremiah said. "It's sure been an unforgettable summer. Not so much for the tragic loss of my brother, but also for the reuniting of me and my nephew, Trevor Hodge. I knew nothing about Trevor until I saw him graduate from college back in May. I learned that he's a pretty smart boy, earnin' honors and getting fancy words printed by his name in the graduation announcement. Now anyone who knows me knows that a bunch of fancy words on paper don't amount to nothin' until a man has shown his real character. Well I'm here to tell you that this summer I've got to know a lot about this young man's character, and for what he's brought to me and our family I'll say that I'm proud to call him my nephew. And if

Jettie were here today, there is no doubt in my mind that he'd be proud to call him his son."

Short applause.

"I've watched him and helped him train so he could come here tonight and pay tribute to his father. He's got smarts, but most of all he's got courage, and ladies and gentlemen, those are the traits of a true cowboy."

The crowd applauded and Jeremiah looked at me and held up the microphone. I walked across the arena—my spurs jingled and the chaps rubbed together between my legs—and the crowd stood and enhanced their applause with whistles and cheers. I had to thank them several times before they quieted enough for me to speak.

"I can't thank you all enough for coming out here tonight to show your support, or for the most part your love for Jettie. I've been here the better part of two months, spending time with my uncle Jeremiah, getting to know him and his wife Jodie, but most of all I've been able to learn a little about who my father was. Standing here now I can tell you that the only regret I have is not having come here before this summer and gotten to know Jettie before he died."

I found my mother in the crowd.

"But it's nothing I blame anyone for. It's just one of life's many circumstances that makes us become who we are. Well, I'm certainly not a bull rider. This summer I've met a lot of men who are, and I can only say that they are some of the most courageous men I've ever met. They carry with them a level of professionalism that can only be envied and respected by anyone who steps forward in this world to do something spectacular.

"Many of you may be wondering why I'm doing this. Well maybe you can answer that by asking yourselves why you came here tonight. I suppose there's a few of you that figure there's a chance you'll see a city boy get his head bashed in by a bull. But I know that like me you've learned to love and respect a man who was known for his high standards. This is my way of telling him I'm proud of who he was, and you being here says the same thing."

More applause.

"Now, just like any cowboy who mounts a bull, I can't guarantee how long I'll stay on. But one promise I can make, for you and for Jettie, is a guarantee, that after I get on that bull, I will come out of that chute like a jet, and ride with the pride of twenty spirited cowboys."

The crowd stood and cheered.

I thanked them and waved my hat, and knew now that all I could do was turn around and head for the chute and pray for the opportunity to hear those applause again.

THIRTY-SEVEN

After the applause died down the arena grew uncomfortably quiet. Denny rode his horse over to the chute and peeked in. I straddled the fence above Cyclone while Jeremiah and crew assembled the gear. Buddy and Tate stood next to Paul Baldwin with their feet on the bottom rail of the gate and watched the preparation, their jester faces brilliant against the western sun that cut through the corral behind us.

I looked up and out to the crowd. "Weird silence."

Buddy looked behind him then nodded at Tate. "Maybe we better go occupy their minds a little."

Denny turned to go with them, then looked back at me. "You never did tell me what music you wanted."

"I have no idea. What did Jettie like?"

Jeremiah dropped the rigging down over the bull. "He never liked music. Ruined his concentration. The cheering of the crowd gave him his energy."

"Then let's keep it authentic."

Denny grinned then nodded and rode away.

Buddy put on a headset microphone and talked to the crowd. Denny joined him in a canned act, where all he had to do was let Buddy do the talking while he responded from horseback. It was a mock western gunfight between Buddy and Tate that was silly, nonetheless, but had the crowd laughing, and for me it served its purpose well.

Jeremiah motioned with his hand for me to sit down on the bull. I took a deep breath and lowered myself onto its back. The animal grunted and slammed its massive body against the rails pinning my right leg. I grimaced and tried to rise up but couldn't. Jeremiah jabbed his fist through the fence and repeatedly punched the bull's rump and Jason slapped its back in the same manner. The bull responded angrily and squirmed enough to free my leg. I let out a large breath.

"You all right?" Jeremiah asked.

I nodded. "Let's go."

He winked at Jason. "Don't even have the rope in his hands and he's already hung up."

Jason grinned, the snuff in his lower lip slightly exposed.

Jeremiah helped me tie on my glove while Jason put the finishing touches on the flank strap. The bull continued to squirm and grunt and blow heavily through his nose. I held a piece of the leather string in my teeth, drawing it tight around my wrist while Jeremiah secured it with a knot.

"How's it going?" Someone asked from behind me. I turned my head to find Boyd in a straw cowboy hat and dark sunglasses looking through the fence.

He climbed up two rails then swung a leg over and straddled the fence. He removed his sunglasses and put them in a shirt pocket and glanced down at the rigging.

"You need some help with that?"

I looked at Jeremiah, whose return stare, I'm sure, was almost as staggering as mine. I nodded and he handed Boyd the flat, plaited rope.

I put my hand under the handle and Boyd wrapped the rope around several times.

"How's that feel?" he asked.

I shook my head. "Tighter."

I opened up my hand and he pulled the rope loose then wrapped it again. It was better this time.

"So what's he gonna do?" he asked.

"I think he's gonna spin."

"What makes you so sure?"

"Well, if he don't, then I can sure be better prepared for the sunfish."

He grinned and patted me on the shoulder. "That's using your head, cowboy."

I glanced out into the arena and saw Jason fall to the ground. Buddy blew at his finger like blowing smoke from a gun and the crowd laughed. Denny looked back at me and I nodded, then he asked the crowd for a round of applause for Buddy Wells and company. They did, and then he asked them if they were ready for some good old-fashioned bull riding. This made them stand and cheer louder.

Paul climbed down into the arena and stood at the end of the gate. Buddy and Jason positioned themselves and faced me. The crowd grew quiet again and I looked down upon the bull, watched it raise and lower its head and snort into the dust. I thought back to my first ride on the mechanical bull, and how I made myself believe it was just a Tilt-A-Whirl ride, and then to Big Banana, and Bloody Mary, and how I had learned their moves. But these reflections didn't provide me with the strength I longed for. I searched for it in the crowd, from the people of Spiro, Jodie, my grandparents, but could only see their own confidence—a gift for me, I presumed, or maybe just their desire to be fulfilled by a spectacle that I had sold them on. Then I saw my mom, who could relay nothing but fear. Not so much for the physical dangers that lay ahead of me, but for all that the ride represented: a possible finale to years of unanswered dreams.

The look from Bella was neither of fear or confidence, but possibly one of uncertainty, not knowing where to turn, wondering what answers the outcome of the ride might bring to her as well. This was the feeling I understood most.

All I had left were the images of my summer in Oklahoma, of the family I've come to know and the father that never had his chance. From my images of him—the tiny house, old pickup, hats, boots, and belt buckles—I found the strength to look at Paul and give him the nod.

Unlike his trademark name, Cyclone went straight out of the chute bucking high. I had prepared for a spin left but its backside went right, only slightly, causing me to overestimate my balance and slide off on the right side. My hat fell off and I hung there, my left leg stretched over the bull's back and my hand caught in the rigging, but the bull sunfished to the left and the force pulled me back over to an almost upright position.

During the near fall all I could hear was Cyclone's hooves pounding into the dirt, when now my critical gift of luck had brought on a roar of applause that helped me realize I was still in the game. But my benefit was Cyclone's loss, and what he couldn't accomplish with a toss he tried with a swift spin. But I sat there, upright and perfect, free hand above me, spurs jabbing into the flanks, all in a spinning blur.

The noise of the crowd suddenly muffled, as if something inside my head had turned them down, shut them out, and all I could hear was the sound of a whining, whistling wind. Though the spinning seemed to grow faster, my body felt locked and no more troubled, and the blistery air became more like a soft, pleasant whisper but still very surreal. I wasn't sure what I was experiencing, whether it was just something in my head or whether the spirit of Jettie Hodge was casting itself around me. Whatever the case, there was no other desire within me other than to simply let it happen.

The sound of the cheering crowd faded back in and then came the whistle. I let go of the handle and fell to my hands and feet and eventually to my side. I turned my head and watched Cyclone continue to buck, the rigging on the dusty ground below its feet, and Buddy and Tate scrambling to lure it out of the arena. But it stopped less than twenty feet away and turned its head toward me. I rose slowly to my feet as it lowered its head and blew into the dirt. I didn't move.

Buddy came around and yelled but the bull gave him only a short glance then looked back at me. Buddy yelled again and waved his arms but the bull stood firm. I don't know why it stared in such a way, but it appeared to be in a state of defeat. One that seemed somewhat in wonder, or possibly out of respect. For whatever reason, it had stared enough, and along with Buddy's waving arms turned and trotted through the gate and out of the arena. Now I felt I could breath, and let out a long relieving breath, then turned to face the cheering crowd.

THIRTY-EIGHT

waved shyly to the crowd as they stood and applauded and was suddenly rushed by Buddy, who hugged me and laughed, and Denny who had dismounted and grabbed my hand and shook it firmly, and Jeremiah who also hugged me and lifted me off the ground.

"I knew you'd do it!" he said.

"You did?"

"No doubt in my mind."

"Well, thanks for the confidence."

"No, Trevor, thank you for a great summer. Kid, you made Oklahoma smile."

He stood beside me and put his arm around my neck. Tate and Jason and Paul were the next ones to arrive and shake my hand and offer congratulations. Then Boyd, who stared for a moment and grinned then gave me my hat and extended his hand.

I returned a firm shake.

"You did good," he said. "You should try for the finals. You'd have a good chance."

"That might be stretching it a bit."

He patted my shoulder and I looked back out into the crowd. Buddy grabbed one of my arms and held it up for me. Jeremiah did the same with the other. The crowd clapped above their heads and cheered louder and I could even see tears in some of their eyes. I looked all around me, and too familiar was the scene of everyone applauding. The clowns and the cowboys, all recognizable faces, smiling and cheering, only this time there was no disapproval. Everyone, including Boyd, seemed satisfied. And my mother, though her face was wet from tears, she had removed her sunglasses and applauded joyfully.

I ventured to the outside of the arena and into a bombardment of laudatory handshakes and pats on the shoulder. Eileen worked her way through the crowd and kissed me firmly on the lips.

"That was one of the sexiest thangs I ever saw," she said, behind breath that smelled like a mix of peppermint and beer.

Luckily, I was able to work away from her through the crowd. Grandpa found me and grabbed my hand. "That was some ride, Trev. Your pa would have been proud."

"Thanks, Grandpa."

Grandma hugged me, too, then Jodie stepped forward and kissed me on the cheek.

"You're a special young man, Trevor Hodge."

"Thanks, Jodie."

She handed me a package wrapped like a gift in brown kraft paper, and the paper felt dusty and smelled old.

"What's this?" I asked.

"Something your mom wanted me to bring to you."

"My mom?"

I sought Mom out through the crowd, and when I saw her she smiled at me. I went to her and she clung to me as though I had just returned from a long journey.

"I'm so sorry, Trevor."

"I know."

She pushed away and looked into my eyes. "Will you ever forgive me?"

"I'm not sure there's anything to forgive."

"How about for being a bad mother?"

"No, you were never that."

"Wasn't I?"

"Things happen, Mom. It's behind us now."

"You know, I read all those letters. I don't think they would have had the same impact then as they did now."

"Why do you say that?"

"The years gone by have provided a lot more time to think."

"Yeah, I suppose you're right."

"And I saw the copy of the will."

"Oh—yeah."

"That was real generous of him."

"Nothing like putting a little money back for your son's education, right?"

"You deserve it, Trevor."

"Thanks, Mom."

"You know, I called Jodie today and she invited me out to the ranch this afternoon. We sat on the deck and drank lemonade. I haven't had lemonade that good in twenty-five years. We talked about the years past, and I shared with her what I read in the letters. She said that spring Jettie came to her and gave her that package. He said that maybe her boys could get some use out of it."

I looked down at the package that Jodie had given me. "*This* package?"

"She said she didn't feel right about giving it to her boys so she put it in a box and put it in the attic. Said she'd forgot all about it until now."

I studied it closely, found a taped end, pulled it open then pulled the paper off. It was a replica of a red and gray Massy Ferguson tractor still in its original box and open in the front displaying its detailed features. It was just like Jettie's and just like the letter had said.

Tears filled my eyes until I could barely see.

"So you got your Christmas present after all," Mom said.

I closed my eyes and held her again.

"Thanks, Mom."

She squeezed me tighter. "No, Trevor, thank you."

My chin still on Mom's shoulder, I opened my eyes and noticed Bella at the end of the arena, leaning against the passenger side of her car.

"Mom, will you excuse me a minute?"

She turned and followed my gaze. "Looks like I better."

I wove through the crowd toward the red Mustang. When the crowd ended, I stopped and looked at her. The setting sun put a special glow on her face and gleam in her eyes. I walked slowly toward her, absorbing every inch of her beauty along the way.

"Hi," I said.

"Nice ride."

"Thanks."

She looked down at the tractor. "New toy?"

"Yeah, well, kind of old, actually."

I looked in her eyes and searched for the right words. "I'm real glad you came."

"Me, too."

"So where are you headed now?"

She glanced over her shoulder and down the road. "Thinking about going out to The Oasis. There's a band playing out there tonight."

"By yourself?"

"Yeah, I do that sometimes."

"Oh."

"What about you? Where are you headed?"

"Haven't gave it much thought, really."

"Maybe you should travel the circuit. Try for the finals."

I laughed. "No, I don't think so."

"Why not? You have the talent."

"Talent is one thing, but the love for it is another. Besides that, I'm a numbers man. I didn't go to college four years for nothing."

This made her laugh. "Probably a good choice."

"I hope so."

We stared silently for a moment.

"Well, good luck to you," she said.

"You, too."

She came to me and offered a short embrace then a kiss on the cheek. When she let go of me and stepped away a sudden lonely fear swept through me, and grew worse as she walked around to the driver side of her car.

She grabbed the door handle then suddenly let go. When she looked up at me I wondered whether she could read the desire in my eyes.

"You know," she said, "if you don't have any plans, you should come out to The Oasis. I hear it's a really good band."

The relief inside of me was immeasurable, as was the way her eyes smiled at me.

"I'd like that."

"Then what are you waiting for? Get in, cowboy."

I couldn't remember ever receiving such a grand invitation, nor a better reward after having finished something so essential to my future.

I grabbed the handle to the car door, but before opening it I turned and looked again at the arena and the aftereffects of a special night, one that possibly would be remembered in Spiro for years to come, but more so, as a final mark on the formal education of Trevor Hodge. Well, maybe it wasn't that formal, but at least I could walk away with a sense of accomplishment, or more importantly, a better understanding of who I really was. It made me think back to the college commencement, and how Ernie and I stood out in the lawn after the ceremony wearing the long blue commencement gowns and gold ropes, and how clean everything was. Wow, how different I looked now. Fancy chaps and boots with jingling spurs and a straw cowboy hat, all soiled by arena dirt. But it seemed only appropriate, because like the sharp contrast in apparel, so was the level of learning I had received here.

I looked down at the straw cowboy hat in my hand then looked toward the sunset sky, and suddenly realized there was only one way to finalize such an event in my life. From the bottom of my vocal chords I found a perfect "yee-haa," then tossed my hat into the air and celebrated the end of a perfect summer.